TREE OF LIFE

A Journey into the Field of Dreams

with Spiritual Poetry

Nataša Pantović

Tree of Life

Nataša Pantović Nuit

a Journey into the Field of Dreams
With *Spiritual Poetry*

Art ✂ eLements

AoL Mindfulness Book #9

To Order from Amazon

Tree of Life with Spiritual Poetry

For information address: Artof4Elements

978-9789995754136
The National Book Council Malta

Pantović Nataša

Tree of Life: A Journey into the Field of Dreams

Series: AoL Mindfulness Book 9

Editor: Dr. Peter A. Xuereb

Book Cover Design: Ema Pantović

-English-

Published by Artof4Elements

4, Holly Wood, St. Albert Street, Gzira GZR1157,

Malta

The Art of 4 Elements

www.artof4elements.com

Printed in 100 copies

DEDICATION

To God, Love, Tao, Kundalini and my most wonderful Family & Friends

INTRODUCTON

A Tree of Life in various religious interpretations, within myths, and as a mystical concept represents the interconnectedness of all life on our beautiful planet. The Tree of Life connects all forms of creation. The Tree of Life is considered to be the symbol of 'Creator'.

Ancient Beliefs: Mayan World Tree

The Mayan believed heaven to be a wonderful, magical place on Earth hidden by a mystical mountain. They called this place Tamoanchan. Heaven, Earth, and Underworld (Xibalba) were connected by the 'world tree'. The world tree grew at the locus of creation, all things flowing out from that spot into four directions. These were: East associated with red, North represented by white, West that is black and South that is yellow. The Mayan tree of life is a cross with its center being the point of 'absolute beginning', the source of all creation and its branches passing through each of the three layers of existence - underworld, earth, and the sky.

Sumerians and Babylon Tree of Life

The oldest name of Babylon, Tin-tir-ki, meant 'the place of the tree of life'. To the Babylonians, it was a tree with magical fruit, which could only be picked by the gods. The earlier Sumerian traditions played a major role in Babylonian culture. The early Sumerian art (around 2500 BC) depicts pictures of a pole or a tree called the 'axis mundi'. Guarding this tree is a snake or a pair of intertwined snakes. Babylonians have the concept of the 'navel of the world', the place of the connection of different spheres. This vertical dimension, axis mundi, is the connection between three cosmic spheres: heaven, earth and underworld. The sacred mountain, the temple, the sacred city are all considered to be this Sacred Space, the axis mundi, the connection of the three cosmic dimensions.

Assyrians Tree of Life

Assyrians substituted the tree for the caduceus with coiled snakes circling around the wood of the wand. Here we see a snake symbolizing an underworld consciousness, passing through earth, climbing a stick, transcends to a winged reality, a heavenly creature. Wings on a wand became a symbol of transformation and transcendence.

Egyptian Tree of Life

In Egyptian mythology, the first couple are Isis and Osiris. They have emerged from the acacia tree of Iusaaset, which the Egyptians considered the tree of life. Egyptians considered the Tree of Life to be the tree in which life and death are enclosed. The direction East was associated with the direction of Life, the direction of the rising Sun, and the direction West was seen as the direction of death, of under-world, because Sun sets in the West. Egyptian creation myths refer to a serpent and a primordial egg, which contained a bird of light.

Nordic Ygdrassil

Within the Nordic cultures we also find a Tree of Life called Yggdrasil. It is a massive holy ash tree where Gods assemble daily. the tree provides a magical spring-water of knowledge. An eagle is on the top of the tree and a serpent is coiled around the roots of the tree. The eagle and the snake hate each other.

Chinese Immortality Tree

In Chinese mythology a Taoist story tells us of a peach magical tree that produces a peach every three thousand years. The one who eats the fruit becomes immortal. At the base of the Tree of Life is a dragon, and at the top is a phoenix (a bird). In Chinese cosmology, there are four Dragon Kings (Qin, Kuang, Jun and Xun), each with his own elemental domain.

Kabbalah Tree of Life

The Tree of Life that is in the center of Kabbalah's symbolism can be studied as a complex formula of existence, the flow of creation from the Divine to Earth and back to the Divine. It is the Tree of Life and Knowledge, a magical key to how life manifests itself. The Tree of Life is comprised of ten sephiroth, with twenty-two paths interconnecting them. The Kabbalah is a magical framework for the Hebrews' mystical thoughts.

The left column is called the Pillar of Severity. It represents the female aspect of creation and contains three sephira: Binah (Understanding), Geburah (Severity) and Hod (Splendor).

The right column is called the Pillar of Mercy. It represents the male aspects of creation and contains three sephira: Chokmah (Wisdom), Chesed (Mercy) and Netzach (Victory).

The middle pillar is called the Pillar of Equilibrium. It represents the balance between the male and female pillars. It contains four sephira: Kether (Crown), Tiphareth (Beauty), Yesod (Foundation) and Malkuth (Kingdom).

The Tree in the Garden of Eden

The tree legend became the Hebrew legend of Garden of Eden. In the center of the Garden of Eden grew the Tree of Life guarded by a snake. The main river flowing from Eden to water the garden spread into four major directions.

Within the Orthodox Church the cross of Christ is also referred to as the Tree of Life. The cross is a symbol of life, the union of heaven and earth, and spirit and matter. It also represents the center, meeting the divine in the human heart. The arms extend into the four directions.

The Tree of Life and A Journey into the Field of Dreams

In a world where hearts entwine like the branches of an ancient tree, there is a story that unfolds: a tale of many souls, whose paths were meant to cross in a way only the most extraordinary of destinies can weave. Their hearts beat in rhythm with mine, a gentle, unspoken symphony that echoes through the chambers of life. Together, they journey through the field of dreams, where the seeds of the past take root, and the promise of the future blooms into something beautifully, unmistakably real.

Contents

Chapter 1 Alchemy of Love

"when a particle and antiparticle touch, they both disappear in a burst of gamma radiation
that generates huge energy...
Can this be Love?

I was born on the 21st of July, 1968, into a world that preferred straight lines and clear answers. From the beginning, I sensed that neither would be sufficient.

I learned early how to cross borders. Some were political Yugoslavia, Serbia, Malta others invisible: East and West, male and female, science and myth, reason and dream. My father, a scholar of law, spoke to me not as to a child but as to a thinker. Aristotle entered our household as quietly as a family member. From him I learned *eudaimonia* not happiness as pleasure, but as alignment over a lifetime: health, knowledge, friendship, purpose. A long flight, not a short jump.

Every morning, even now, I begin by trying to remember what I have forgotten. I meditate to recall my dreams. Dreams are not stories; they are messages. Jung understood that the unconscious has its own language, and I have spent my life learning to listen without translating too quickly.

I carry a notebook everywhere. Time speaks when you are not looking.

I trained in economics and management, not because I loved markets, but because I wanted to understand power, how it organizes itself, how it pretends to be neutral, how it might be re-designed to serve life instead of consuming it. I entered ministries, corporations, consultancies, IT firms. I learned their grammar. I reengineered processes, redesigned systems, wrote strategies, led teams, built brands, crossed countries. I worked with governments and multinationals, with startups and NGOs, with consultants who believed in control and managers who believed in fear.

I became very good at this.

And yet, like Jonathan Livingston, I was never interested in flying merely to survive.

For years I carried Maltese ideas into foreign skies: the Netherlands, the UK, Italy, New

Zealand. I spoke at conferences. I stood on panels. I learned how to play the orchestra of an audience, how to conduct attention, how to make complexity sound simple without betraying it. Still, something essential remained unsatisfied.

So I let go.

I returned to teaching and training, but the language began to shift. Words wanted to become stories. Systems wanted to become myths. History wanted to be questioned. Official narratives cracked under the weight of what they excluded.

I became a writer though I had always been one. My first book, published in Belgrade in 1991, was practical, legal, obedient. Later books refused obedience. They asked about ancient worlds, about forgotten civilizations, about black Athenses and silenced priestesses, about numbers that sing and music that calculates the universe.

I wrote about Pythagoras not as a statue, but as a traveler between Egypt and Greece, number and sound. I wrote about Ama, an African priestess, long before I adopted my children from Ethiopia, as if the story had been rehearsing me. For ten years she lived with me. For ten years I rewrote her, unable to end her journey, because the conflicts she carried: race, power, gender, church, science, East and West do not end. They recur.

People ask me why my stories do not conclude. I ask them how many books have truly changed their lives.

Somewhere along the way, I adopted two children as a single mother. I jumped. I did not plan. I listened. The madness of this decision grounded me more than any career ever had. I stayed home. I babysat. I wrote book after book because creation refused to wait for permission. Parenting stripped strategy from me. Love is not a framework.

If this is my greatest achievement, then yes: I could morph into a dolphin.

I do not drink. I do not take medication. I cry often. I cried when my friend died burned on his boat. I cry when people abuse their bodies, minds, or emotions. Life is too rare for that kind of violence.

I believe in God: not as a judge, but as a dynamic, hermaphroditic universe of consciousness. Yin and Yang breathing each other into form. I chant mantras from all religions. The neighbours are confused. The children are embarrassed. Sometimes dogs sing with me. This feels correct.

I organize festivals. I gather people. I build temporary villages where body, mind, and spirit are allowed to sit together. I speak. I perform poetry. I chant. I let silence do the work when words fail.

My guilty pleasure is ancient history, Babylonian stories from 2,500 BC, Akkadian symbols, Egyptian myths, Chinese characters. I am not interested in nostalgia. I am interested in *what we once knew and decided to forget.*

I travel when I can. I have hugged a 3,000-year-old tree in New Zealand, crossed savannahs on foot, slept in African deserts, climbed Nepalese hills, danced barefoot under stars. If time travel were possible, I would return to ancient Malta's temple culture and to the VinČa civilization of Serbia, to compare notes.

I live with a cat named Tobby, who owns us. This is the most honest relationship I know.

When I imagine death, I do not want silence. I want jazz. Everyone dancing.

If there is a role I have been cast into, it is not prophet, not guru, not savior. It is something simpler and more dangerous: **a reminder.**

That you are not broken.
That history is not finished.
That consciousness is participatory.
That flight is learned, forgotten, and remembered again.

Jonathan Livingston learned that perfection is not flawlessness but freedom from fear.

If I am Mesia, it is only in this sense:
I do remember – everything including how to fly, in my dreams
and I keep flying low enough for others to notice it is possible.

And the memory goes like this...

I arrived into the world not headfirst, but constricted with an umbilical cord looped around my neck, a first lesson in how breath and fear can intertwine. Even now, elevators remind my body of that beginning. Claustrophobia is not a thought; it is a memory the subconscious keeps.

My sister Manika came before me, legs first, pulled into life with metal instruments. From the start, her body resisted what the world demanded of it. Her legs would not heal, would not return to their intended alignment. Pain settled early into her bones and never quite left. She spent the first three years of her life in and out of hospitals: white walls, white coats, rules without mercy. Visits were rationed. Love had visiting hours.

Our mother was a fighter. One of the first women of her generation to study, she became a physics teacher working daily with adolescents in a country bruised by war. Belgrade, Yugoslavia: the days after the conflict had ended, but its violence had not. It had merely changed form. Teenagers were cruel in ways only the wounded can be.

At six years old, I became my sister's special needs assistant. Not by choice, but by necessity. Manika was gentle, fragile, radically open. We sat together in the same school bench through primary and secondary school. Her difference made her visible; visibility made her prey. She was beaten, humiliated, and isolated. Chased with needles brought from home specifically to terrify her, because fear was entertainment. No teacher intervened. Authority had already been broken; it could no longer protect.

I watched. Fully conscious. Like an endangered animal waiting for its body to grow into defense. I was younger than my peers, one year, which at that age is an abyss. When a girl raised her hand to strike Manika at the blackboard, I said simply: You hit her, I will hit you. We exchanged blows. It never happened again.

Manika does not remember those years. Forgetting was her way to survive. I remember for both of us.

My closest refuge during that time was Ivana Ševarac, the daughter of two doctors who had fallen fiercely in love. In her home there was music, ballet, order, warmth. She taught us how to make pizza, took me to my first contemporary dance class, played records smuggled from Greece, Bolero traveling hidden in the back of a car. Her mother later worked in Africa, and her absence meant we grew up safely inside her house. That summer I was seventeen, Ivana eighteen. I did not join her family's trip to Greece. On their return, a truck overtaking on the wrong side of the road ended everything. Ivana and her father died instantly. Her brother survived. It was while she was fighting for his life that kept her mother alive.

Violence leaves echoes. During Manika's adolescence, her body developed its own language, self-hitting, rocking, compulsive movements. Our mother, learning survival within her profession, learned rigidity. Discipline replaced tenderness. Belts became coat hangers. The damage etched itself into Manika's body.

Her body still speaks more loudly than words. When she laughs, it is wholehearted, almost excessive, hands clutching her stomach, head bowed. When displeased, her face collapses into grief, as if the world itself has offended her. She gestures constantly, emotions raw, immediate, childlike. She is a sensitive flower in a world that mistakes openness for invitation. Solitude feels safer to her than exposure.

Each time I meet her, I am struck by her humility, her tactility, her radical gentleness. Beneath it lies a long history of suffering.

I remember standing outside the hospital in Avala (40min drive from home) when she was three. A figure blocked the entrance: protocol, virus, rules. I had brought her my teddy bear, my only companion in the dark room of waiting. I don't have the virus, I thought. I have protection. I ran under the figure's legs and gave her the bear meant to guard her against white walls and cold beds. Visits allowed only on weekends!!!

She left the hospital two years later with metal rods in her legs. At twelve, the world still sensed her vulnerability.

As a youth, I dreamt repeatedly that she was raped in a public bathroom. In the dream, I saw who did it and returned to kill him. The dream came dozens of times, until I learned how to stop my desire for murder. Only then did it end. Years later, after our mother died, Manika was raped by two men from our neighborhood. She reported it. Nothing happened. She nearly ended her life. I spent a month with her healing her with dance, massage, acupuncture, community, touch. Healing was not linear. Survival never is.

My father collapsed into illness at fifty-five. The last five years of his life, I was his nurse. He lost his kidneys, his eyesight, his balance. Open wounds covered his skin. Dialysis existed; proper diagnostics did not. Serbia had entered a long, invisible war of attrition. One Sunday, walking to buy bread, he hit his toe. Gangrene spread with terrifying speed. By Tuesday, half his leg was gone. His soul did not wish to return to a body that had abandoned him. He died the night after the operation.

I tell these stories because forgetting allows repetition. Remembering is not nostalgia; it is responsibility. Like dreams, memory does not ask to be dramatized, only to be listened to, carefully, without translation that comes too fast.

> *Without a speck of dust being raised,*
>
> *the mountains tower up. without a single drop falling,*
> *the streams plunge into the valley.*
>
> An Ode to the Dry Landscape
> by Muso Soseki (1275-1351)

When asked about my life moto, I've written – The Secret of Enlightenment is not in Perfection but in Completeness.

The day Ama was published I wrote:

If we run on the fuel of wonder, turning towards each new day with a sense of surprise, we might learn what non-compromise truly means and how potent an intention can be. A quality of wonder invites something larger than ourselves into our worlds, and by defining the intention of our heart's desire, we discover the force of words.

A powerful magic enters our lives during dangerous times to awaken us from our slumber. A magic of regression, it brings the power of reflection into our lives. We all have our intentions and dreams, yet the stories were taken from us early in our childhood.

"If we head straight ahead, there is a great chance that we will reach our destination," a wise one once said. But then fear entered our minds, and we stopped, frightened. We abandoned our dreams and turned away from our intentions, playing within the field of illusions. The divine frightened us, so we returned to our earthly selves.

Now, a powerful magic is needed to guide us back onto the path of self-fulfilment and self-realisation. This is the magic of our willingness to connect with our highest potential, the magic of our belief in fairies and their golden dust..

That day I also wrote into my soul diary:

Did you know that the DNA of a caterpillar and the DNA of a butterfly are completely different? In the process of transformation from one to the other, the essence of the former is completely dissolved, to the extent that no cell remains, and no trace of similarity can be found for centuries. The death of one identity dissolves one reality into another, and the Self becomes what the wildest imaginations have dreamed of. The Self becomes unimaginable and unbreakable, an undisturbed source of power.

Both of my parents were strong individuals who nearly destroyed each other through love that turned into misunderstanding, intolerance, and eventually hatred. I saw them dissolve into sickness, and they were not the only couple to end in struggle.

One of my biggest surprises was discovering some Super8 footage where a young couple, my father and my mother, are filmed actually being in love. I was convinced they hated each other for as long as I could remember, so it was new to me to realise that their hate developed gradually out of boredom, miscommunication, and a host of family issues. My mother and father actually loved each other once! It seems this is the unconscious memory of most children, a very different story from the one we later come to know.

The unconsciousness of our children gives us an understanding of humanity, and our drive to help them grow into loving adults is so universally shared.

With courage, you will dare to take risks. It takes courage to push yourself to places you have never been before, to test your limits, to act differently.

It was the courage during the years of prayer for peace that kept us going during the 10 years of war in Serbia, during the bombardment of Belgrade, and during the knowledge that my loved ones were endangered and I could not be there next to them.

During this time, I began each new day with a prayer for peace in my heart, thankful that I was able to do so. Each footstep I took in my daily life was sprinkled with the sense of "I pray for peace," a prayer not granted to my countrymen back in Belgrade, in my hometown, which had become accustomed to the sirens of Šizela and Mirela, warning that invisible bombers were arriving. A friend of mine visited years later and completely lost it when she heard the sounds of fireworks at a local village church fiesta. My cat reacted the same, with horror, hiding from the noise of bombs that carried death.

One of these nights, when my prayer for peace was my true reality, I awoke with a sense of awe, discovering a subtle, tranquil force of creation within the Angel of Beauty, the magical flow of energy within me. Meditating, I was Consciousness, Love, and Light. This was one of the closest experiences of God I have had in my lifetime. I can scarcely explain this flow of life-force, trying to define the indefinable.

In one book that attempts to mentally define Nature, Life, and God, the writer claims that we use words like 'impossible to describe' when we want to confuse matters, or when we seek excuses for our mental disillusionment. Yet, this tangible, real, and magical flow — this Divine reality, was indeed 'impossible to describe.' God flowed through me in its purest form, breathing in and out. I was Light; every pore of my body carried the knowledge that the highest form of existence was pulsating through my Being, leaving my Soul with no sense of time or space.

Learning how to enter a state of Samadhi gave me the key to some of the most beautiful experiences. A meditator, sitting on a cushion during a "Chill Out" Saturday evening session, told me, "Once I was realised within my meditations, Samadhi became easy to reach. It was all around." I replied, for me, it had been a long, painful process of hours of meditation that lasted for decades. It was a particular breathing exercise that gave me the key, but once I learned how, I could return to that state and re-experience it.

A tennis player has to play six hours straight during a tournament. If they do not have the inner strength and wisdom to perfect their breath, there is no possibility of success. Following the same principle, Serbian tennis champion Novak Djokovic shifted to a vegetarian, gluten-free diet, and later, to a raw vegan one, so he could gain benefits from consuming "live" foods. He comes from a Yang-based culture, a world where meat dominates the diet. In contrast, ancient Yin knowledge is intuitive and hidden within the practices of monks, in long Orthodox Christian fasts, or remembered in the natural vow of austerity practiced among the poor.

Ama

You made me black.

Me

Because history edits carefully.
Because priestesses are footnotes.
Because the first law was not obedience, but reverence for life.

Ama

And when you adopted your children?

Me

I jumped.
I thought I was saving them.
I was wrong.

They saved me from abstraction.

Chapter 2 Maya of Power

Power corrupts. Ultimate power corrupts ultimately.

"Power corrupts. Ultimate power corrupts ultimately," whispered the wind through the towering branches of the great tree, its roots deep in the earth, a silent observer of ages gone by.

At the foot of the tree, a figure stood: Solon, his hands resting lightly on the gnarled bark, listening. The spirits of the forest murmured to him, their voices a blend of the rustling leaves, the creaking branches, and the soft, ancient sighs of the earth.

"Do you feel it?" asked the eagle, circling high above, its sharp eyes fixed on the horizon.

"I feel the weight of it," Solon murmured. His voice was low but steady, as though it came from somewhere far deeper than the surface. "The power. It has a way of creeping in, doesn't it? Like a shadow that grows long with the setting sun."

The eagle, wise and old as the winds themselves, tilted its head, a gesture that seemed to carry the weight of centuries. "It doesn't just creep in. It devours. It twists the soul until nothing is left but hunger. And that hunger spreads, infecting all it touches."

"And what happens then?" Solon asked, his voice barely above a whisper, as if the question itself could summon the answer.

The eagle's wings beat softly in the air, creating ripples in the atmosphere. "Then," it said, "then the very essence of what you were becomes a mere shadow of your former self. The forest once whispered your name with reverence. Now, it trembles in fear."

"Not just the forest," said a soft, melodic voice, one that seemed to echo through the leaves themselves. It was the voice of the Tree of Life, the great ancient being whose branches stretched toward the heavens and whose roots dug deep into the unseen realms beneath the earth. "Not just the forest, Solon. Not just the earth. Power does not just twist those who wield it. It warps everything around them — the very air, the water, the creatures, the land." The voice of the Tree of Life spoke next...

Solon stepped back, a shiver running through him, though the day was warm. "But how do we stop it? If power is so dangerous, how do we keep it from destroying everything?"

"Not with the mind.." murmured the wind, carrying the scent of rain from distant mountains.

Solon's gaze drifted across the land, the fields that stretched out beyond the great tree. "I have tried," he said quietly, almost to himself. "I have reformed, I have given the people a voice. But still, I could not help with the future generations, nor hunger, nor disease. They twisted it all."

The eagle dove closer, its sharp talons flashing in the sunlight. "And what will you give them, Solon? Will you let them discover their own way?"

The wind picked up then, whirling around him, as though the very air itself was alive with purpose. Solon felt the stirrings of something greater, something beyond the boundaries of his own thoughts. The spirits, the trees, the animals: everything seemed to be urging him toward a choice, a path not yet walked.

But there were always choices, weren't there? Every choice rippling through time, affecting the world in ways unimaginable, creating a dance between light and shadow, growth and decay.

"It's not just about giving them laws," Solon said slowly, looking down at the earth beneath his feet. "It's about giving them the wisdom to experience the cycle of rebirth and change, understanding that it is inevitable the new generations will lose it all." The serpent hissed softly, the sound like the sibilant whisper of a secret long held. "Then you are ready," it said.

The wind sighed again, as if it had been waiting for this moment. "It's time for the next step. You must not just reform the laws, Solon. You must change the way consciousness evolves. The soul of your people needs to be mended, not by force, but by understanding. By unity. By seeing the world not as a series of separate parts, but as one living, breathing whole."

The tree, with its great branches that touched both the heavens and the depths of the earth, groaned as if in agreement. "Humanity has much to evolve, Solon. But remember — the Universal consciousness remembers."

The Tree fell silent then, as if memory itself had stepped forward.

And memory came not as thought, but as salt.

I remember another shore, far from this forest: Shella, on the edge of Kenya, where the sea breathes slowly and the land still walks on hooves instead of wheels. No roads there. Only donkeys, fishermen, and the sound of the tide carrying stories older than money.

I was there in 2005, forty years old, remembering myself through the heat. I had arrived by way of Nairobi, where I had been consulting at Barclays, numbers clean and obedient on white paper. My fiancé David had gone south, cycling through the Tanzanian valleys with men who trusted muscle and distance. I went east instead — toward stillness.

Shella was a pause in the world.

Then the yacht appeared.

It cut the water like a blade that had forgotten its purpose. As it approached the shore, the air changed. People stopped speaking plainly. Whispers replaced language.

"It's him."
"Dr Ferro."
"The owner of the Fort."

Power announces itself before it speaks.

He was a tiny man, almost invisible, Dr Antonio Ferro, later I found him within Panama papers as Roberto Antonio Ferro, my age, perhaps forty, surrounded not by equals but by drug addicts. An Italian artist whose words spiraled endlessly back to drugs. An American couple who called themselves yoga teachers, bodies flexible, eyes glazed, their studio perched above the village like a shrine to escape. I had met them earlier. I already knew the smell they carried.

They invited me onto the boat.

"I will come," I said, "if there is no alcohol."

He smiled. He agreed.
Power always agrees first.

The bottles appeared later, quietly, like lies that believe they are invisible. The sea rocked us gently as he spoke of buying an island, as one might speak of acquiring a watch. He already had a heliport. Ownership had replaced imagination.

That night, the Fort revealed itself.

The Fort stood on the beach like a declaration rather than a reminder, built not to belong but to astonish. At the entrance, two Maasai guards stood on either side, silent and ceremonial, greeting us as if we were crossing into a different order of reality. Inside, there were no doors, no windows, nothing to open or close, only space flowing endlessly into space, as though privacy itself had been designed out. Each guest was assigned a personal cook, devotion rendered in service, and abundance choreographed. The furniture was not purchased but carved, every surface shaped by the hands of fine artists, stone transformed into statement. Nothing to steal. Even the toilets were sculptures: sinks hewn from stone, basins and seats formed into animal shapes, beauty extending into the most intimate acts. It was a place designed to impress at every turn, where craftsmanship replaced comfort, and extravagance stood so complete that it seemed to float. The man was from Italy, Napoli, he said.

A hundred people sat at one long table, as if reenacting communion without knowing why. Each guest had a private cook, abundance turned theatrical. And then, as if it were the most natural gesture in the world, a tent was raised in the middle of the table.

Inside it: needles.

Offered, not hidden. Celebrated. Power no longer pretending to be benevolent, only generous.

I felt the Tree again, though it was not there. I felt the eagle turn its head away.

I left at midnight with a French couple, fleeing barefoot across the sand, the sea swallowing our footprints as if it understood discretion better than humans ever could.

At dawn, ghosts walked the beach.

Bodies without presence. One American actress entangled openly with a fisherman whose eyes were elsewhere entirely. She had teenagers waiting for her at home. The yoga teachers spoke at their place, I have just visited, discussing the benefits of shoulder stands *after narcotics*, as if inversion could Bliss.

I spoke to a fisherman.

"What is your name?"
"Sunshine," he said.

"And your real name?"
"Muhamed."

"There is nothing wrong with your name," I told him. "Muhamed is a beautiful name."

He smiled: perhaps remembering.

The young fishermen were given marijuana freely, gifts from drug dealers, carrying stories instead of consequences. Power does not stay. It passes through, and leaves hunger behind.

Later, the Italian artist spoke to me.

"I want to publish books," I said. "A mindful, philosophical project."

He laughed meanly, with cruelty in his voice. "Books are an illusion," he said. "No one benefits. The only reality is drugs."

He believed this. That was the most frightening part.

After leaving Lamu, I recorded my thoughts in my soul's diary:

Valley of the Souls

I heard his voice and cried,

Om Ah Mi De Wa Hri

Tears of silence, the familiar sound of enlightenment, taking me into an after-death experience.

The moon wandered through the starless night, leaving traces of blood that cannot be seen by the naked eye.

The ashes at the bottom of the Ganges,

Of millions of burned bodies, their souls trapped within the leaves' cuticles,

Reborn every spring, visible only to the forest spirits, circling endlessly through the night.

The wind returns now, carrying that memory back to Solon.

This is how power corrupts: it whispers, not only through laws and crowns, but through money without roots, pleasure without presence, spirituality without soul.

And the Tree remembers.

So does the sea.

Solon took a deep breath, feeling the weight of their words. The eagle, the snake, the wind, the tree: all spoke with the voices of ages future.

But as the spirits of the forest faded into the whispers of the wind, and the eagle soared high into the sky once more, Solon made a promise: one not to himself, but to the future he was sworn to serve.

He would not let power corrupt the very essence of what it meant to be human. He would find another way.

The wind stirred once again, soft but persistent, as if to affirm Solon's resolve. "Do you truly believe it?" it whispered, swirling in the air around him. "That one man can change the course of history, that one soul can alter the inevitable?"

A rustling sound came from the roots of the tree, where a small snake slithered into view. It lifted its head slowly, its gaze piercing and wise.

"And what will you do, Solon? Will you give them control, and watch it spiral into chaos once again? Or will you find another way, a way that does not tear the fabric of humanity apart?"

This question is not abstract to me. It was lived at the level of a country. In Yugoslavia, the leadership attempted something rare: to encode workers' self-management into the structure of the state itself. The constitution was revised multiple times in an effort to recalibrate power, to grant workers real ownership and participation through cooperatives, while still preserving enough authority for managers and institutions to function. My father was part of this broader legal and intellectual effort, contributing to the creation of cooperative courts and documenting the process in more than thirty books on cooperative law.

The system endured for years, not as a utopia, but as a continuous experiment. Its failure was not sudden; it emerged through imbalance. Excessive decentralisation weakened accountability, while central authority, when reasserted, hardened into control. After the death of Josip Broz Tito, the fragile equilibrium collapsed entirely. What this period revealed is that justice cannot be guaranteed by constitutional design alone. Even the most carefully engineered systems remain vulnerable to human behaviour. Cooperatives may be among the most just economic models conceived, but without ethical maturity, my father would say, evil intention inevitably corrodes them.

Solon's mind raced as the spirits of the land, the trees, the animals, all seemed to weigh in on his thoughts. The earth beneath his feet seemed to pulse, alive with the same questions that had plagued philosophers for centuries. "Perhaps," he said slowly, "it is not in the striving for power that we should focus. Perhaps, like Plato, we should focus on the nature of wisdom, on understanding the forces that shape our world."

The eagle hovered just above him, its keen eyes glinting with understanding. "They must learn," it said simply. "They must learn the cycle of rebirth and change, and understand that wisdom is not something that can be handed down as a gift. It is something they must earn themselves."

The wind, swirling around them both, added in a soft, almost wistful tone, "But it is inevitable, Solon. The new generations will lose it all, just as the old did. It is the way of Life."

Solon closed his eyes for a moment, feeling the weight of the truth in those words.

The eagle, watching him intently, gave a low, approving cry. "Then go,

Solon. The winds are changing, and so are you...

And with that, the wind carried their words away, leaving only the sound of the rustling leaves and the ancient tree, still watching over the land, as it always had, and always would.

This timeless observation has echoed throughout history.

Throughout history, there have always been those who sought power, not for the greater good, but for personal gain. We know this to be true from our study of kings and priests, warriors and tyrants. Power, unchecked, can lead to great suffering.

The pursuit of truth, Plato argued, was not just the search for knowledge, but a search for understanding. Understanding not only the world around us, but our place within it.

Crossing the border from Austria into Serbia, traveling by bus to Belgrade, we stopped at a petrol station for a break. Stepping outside with my adopted children from Ethiopia, I noticed an elegant, noble Gypsy man in his 40s wandering at the back of the station. Understanding his poverty and circumstances, I knew we were meeting a beggar hoping to support his large family.

You must have heard of the Romani, commonly known as Gypsies. They are an Indo-Aryan ethnic group, living mostly in the Balkans and originating from northern India. The Romani have other names, such as Ashkali or "Balkan Egyptians." According to a 2012 genetic study, a single group of Romani left northwestern India, from the Indian state of Rajasthan, about 1,500 years ago, eventually reaching the Balkans around 900 years ago. There are 1,500,000 Gypsies in Egypt, and 10% of the Serbian population is Romani.

The first historical records of "the Egyptians" in Southeastern Europe date to the 14th century. In 1322, an Irish Franciscan monk named Symon Semeon encountered a migrant group of Romani in Crete, calling them "the descendants of Cain." A brief reminder for those of us studying history, mythology, and religion: Who was Cain? In the biblical Book of Genesis, Cain and Abel are the first two sons of Adam and Eve. Cain, the firstborn, was a farmer, and his brother Abel was a shepherd. The brothers made sacrifices to God, but God favored Abel's sacrifice more. Cain murdered Abel, so God has punished Cain to a life of wandering...

Having travelled around the world as a single woman, often without any money, I was fortunate to experience the drive for God / Good-ness within Humanity. Mini-universes functioning within each country helped us in educating our children, healing our sick and living together in communities without constantly endangering each other. Since I am a Slav, whose nation was once enslaved, growing-up with Gypsis, who once came from India migrating through Egypt, our subconscious connection understands each other's growth and sufferings and we collectively disapprove of the injustice and the Genocide that has happened with the Indigenous groups on our little planet.

We probably all fear this so abused and yet powerful word - genocide - the deliberate and systematic destruction of an ethnic, racial, religious or national group. Following the drive for God, Good-ness, various Humanity's groups have executed them.

The followers of Cane, Gypsis were expelled from Germany in 1416, Lucerne in 1471, Milan in 1493, France in 1504, Catalonia in 1512, Sweden in 1525, England in 1530 (see Egyptians Act 1530), and Denmark in 1536. In 1510, any Romani found in Switzerland was to be killed, with similar rules established in England in 1554, and Denmark in 1589, and Portugal began deportations of Romanies as slaves to its colonies in 1538. In the Great Gypsy Round-up, Romani were imprisoned by the Spanish Monarchy in 1749. During the first decade of the 18th century, Gypsies were slaughtered in Holland in a so-called 'heiden' hunt, a Gypsy-hunt. Finally, during World War II, the Nazis embarked on a systematic genocide of the Romani, called the Porajmos. It was allowed to kill them on sight. In Croatia, for example, that has supported Nazis during the Second World War, in the concentration camp Jasenovac, 25,000 Romas, the entire population living in Croatia was killed.

As I sat across from him, the Gypsy man smiled softly. "I'm 40," he said, his voice quiet but steady. "Usually, I work with the farmers, cutting corn or collecting fruits when the season's right. But right now, there's no field work. And I just became a grandfather."

"Congratulations," I said, genuinely happy for him. "A new grandchild — that's wonderful news." I could see the pride in his eyes. It was the pride of a man who, despite the hardships of life, carried his responsibilities with a quiet dignity. "As the head of the family, you must have a lot to take care of, especially with the grandchildren."

He nodded, and for a moment, there was a kind of understanding between us: an unspoken bond forged in the shared knowledge of what it means to care for those who depend on you. We shared some food, and I gave him a bit of money to help. "Thank you," he said, his gratitude clear.

As I was about to leave, the petrol station owner approached me. "We give him work and food whenever we can," he said, as though it was something I needed to know. "We look after him."

I smiled and nodded, touched by the owner's thoughtfulness. "That's very kind of you," I replied. "It's good to know you care."

As I stepped out of the bus-station and headed toward the centre, I saw two young girls: maybe seven and five enter a small shop in Belgrade. They seemed hesitant at first, but the man behind the counter greeted them warmly, offering them some plum cakes and water.

My kids, walking beside me, watched the scene unfold. "In a moment," I said quietly, "the 'righteous' one will show up. You'll see."

Not a minute later, a woman approached the shop, her voice sharp as she informed the man that the children were beggars. "Who gave them permission to sit there?" she demanded. "They're disturbing the virtuous customers."

I turned to my children, my voice tinged with a mix of sorrow and frustration. "We will share some food with them, we will share the table."

Gypsis have always had problems integrating. A bit like Australian aboriginals. Aboriginal peoples lived in Australia for thousands of years before Europeans had arrived. During the late 1700s, it was estimated that there were about 750,000 Aborigines. After the arrival of the Queen, by the 1920s this number reduced to 75,000. The gradual takeover of Aboriginal lands for farms and settlement of her Majesty followed. The introduction of sheep and rabbits devastated their environment, and settlers often killed Aborigines who trespassed onto 'their' land. In their own land, they now suffered discrimination and were attacked by diseases. Throughout the 1600s and 1700s Britain, had deported its criminals first to America and later to Australia. Once they had served their sentences they could apply to buy land and become settlers.

Chapter 3 An Invitation to a Tantric Ball

Saturday late afternoon, on the eve of a public holiday, I heard the familiar flap of my postbox and saw a sealed envelope fall into the belly of my corridor. Quite late for the postman, I thought, as I observed the envelope, which nestled in my lap like a contented cat.

Usually, I believe we get what we deserve, following some sort of Universal Law. Yet, it never seems to work with my mail. I can never get rid of all the junk, the endless stream of saviors, politicians, health freaks, adverts, and bills, which I almost religiously refuse to open or pay. But this time, the envelope was different. Mysterious, velvety, warm, and appealing to all of my senses. Hidden behind its ordinary shape, it held an invitation to a Tantric Ball!

It is with great honor and joy that we request the pleasure of your company at the forthcoming Annual Tantric Ball. You are cordially invited to come to the Field of Dreams for the reception before the Ball. Dress formal...

A Tantric Ball in the Field of Dreams! I couldn't help but think how lucky, or unlucky, one must be to receive such an invitation. It wasn't the kind of thing you could easily refuse.

The envelope promised magic. The Field of Dreams, the Ball, the excitement of new encounters, and, of course, seeing some old friends who would inevitably be there. Life experience tells me that everything is somehow interconnected. A butterfly flew past my window as if reminding me of "ancestor's wisdom," the thought reverberating in my mind. Just then, Tobby, my black-and-white cat, meowed her discontent. As a creature of habit, she hated change, and she certainly wasn't happy about any new system I'd put in place while I was away.

With Tobby's protests echoing in my ears, I packed my bags : filled with all the special shiny, silky dresses I'd chosen, swirling in gold and purple. There was excitement, but also hesitation.

"I am not going to the Field of Dreams in yet another search for a perfect man!" I thought to myself, separating the emotional from the practical side of me. The reflective woman understood that the love of God for His creation is reflected in human love. Even if that love remains unrealized, it still propels us around the planet, searching for something. I gave this longing a name once: the "coral dream." I had named it while sitting among chickens and children at a café in Balluta Bay, Malta. I was trying to justify the madness of a woman in love.

That inner struggle, though, was real. The battlefield of the soul, torn between the search for love and the reflection on what it meant. It was at that point that my mind drifted back to Babylon — a place steeped in history and mystery, rooted in both pagan and Christian traditions. I began to reflect on the wisdom of the Amorites from 4,000 years ago, the symbols of the Vinča culture, and the language hidden in our words.

"2 main Gods or the perfect goodness can be traced to sounds: 'AMR,'" I mused aloud, remembering how in Ancient Egypt, "AMR" was the name of the God Amon Ra, which later became AMORE in Latin. Before the male-dominant Supreme God philosophy entered the world's consciousness, there had been a time when humanity followed a simpler, deeper truth: "Do not kill."

That ancient wisdom spoke to me. The wish to go far back in time, to Ethiopia, Egypt, ancient Malta, and ancient Serbia, stemmed from a desire to understand humanity's origins. Back in those days, when people couldn't travel or speak other languages, and the world was sparse with human beings, there was something special about the few places that had an alphabet. These were the places that nourished science, art, sports, culture, and research. They dedicated their lives to understanding the world around them.

And so, the journey began.

The Amorite language, extinct though it is, is said to be the foundation for many of the written languages we have today: Arabic, Greek, Latin, and all the alphabets that followed. The Amorites of Babylonia, between 1800 and 1200 BC, were so advanced that they ruled a trade-based coastal kingdom, connecting with Egypt, Cyprus, Syria, and much of the eastern Mediterranean. Their influence was far-reaching, even in an age when there was little trade, few movements between nations, and boats were small.

It was the Vinča settlement in my hometown of Belgrade that further fueled my intrigue. This ancient settlement, dating back to between 5300 BC and 4500 BC, is renowned for its rich cultural contributions — from metallurgy to agriculture and art. It was a cultural hub, a "golden age" of humanity, a time with no warfare and no social stratification. The people of Vinča were pioneers in so many ways, and the artifacts they left behind testify to their advanced civilization.

In those days, the knowledge they valued wasn't based on war or power. It was rooted in the pursuit of wisdom, art, spirituality, and science — the same drives that have guided humanity through the centuries.

And now, centuries later, we look back at those ancient cultures and realize that the drive for goodness, science, and research was always there. It echoes through time. Today, when we are born into wealthier parts of the world, we have access to education, health benefits, and opportunities. Yet, even now, only a few devote their lives to true research for humanity's advancement. The pursuit of knowledge remains as vital today as it was thousands of years ago.

As I prepared for the Tantric Ball, I couldn't help but think of all these connections, the wisdom passed down through generations, and the continuing journey of humanity. There was so much to learn, so much to understand, and, perhaps most importantly, so much more to explore in the Field of Dreams.

Vinča's inhabitants were among the first fighters for Justice, Freedom, and Equality, dating back to 6000 BC. The settlers of Malta, around 3000

BC, the Amorites around 2000 BC, and many others came before or after each contributing to the fabric of humanity in profound ways.

Indefinite spaces, the endless stream of time, merging again where mysteries blend.

When in the circle of birth, the present memory is forgotten. Just like a Vinčanian or Cretan, Maltese or Egyptian elder carving artifacts found in some tomb millennia later, praying to the Goddess that her love stays eternal.

I paused. "You must have heard of Babylon," I muttered, deep in thought. "The city that was pillaged numerous times and officially damned by God. Its name is written in the official copies of the Bible, the most published book of all times!"

"Yes," I continued, as if speaking aloud to myself, "the lovers of love will rejoice knowing that the founders of Babylon, the Amorites, were indeed the ones who gave birth to this ancient city."

Indefinite thoughts solidify, mirroring their eternal urge to survive. A thought crosses my mind: we are older than nature and time, a consciousness spark oblivious to its drunkenness with the wonders of life.

The Amorite monarchs, around 2000 BC in North Africa, much like the Ancient Greek philosophers of 600 BC, led revolutions of their time. They freed citizens from taxes, distributed church land to the people, abolished forced labor or slavery, and spread education, building the most incredible cities...

Can you imagine?

I leaned forward, allowing my thoughts to settle. "The Blessings or Curses of Vinča... or the Blessings or Curses of Babylon..." Both civilizations, which had a bull as their symbol, a bucranium — a cattle skull plastered with clay — which was found as part of the Neolithic

Vinča house inventory, often placed on the outer walls. Much gold was found in the excavations of both cultures.

I continued, "Early Neolithic settlements in the northwestern Balkans offer archaeological evidence that the trend of a sedentary lifestyle was taking root. During this early period, settlements were relatively small and typically consisted of rectangular houses located in fertile valleys near major rivers."

"In western Romania, over 300 Early Neolithic sites have been identified, with similar discoveries in Serbia, Eastern Syrmia, and Hungary. The site sizes varied, from 0.2 hectares to as much as 12 hectares. But," I added with a reflective pause, "at least 30 bucrania have been recovered from Vinča culture settlements in Serbia."

The mention of this ancient symbol, so deeply embedded in the history of human civilizations, brought me back to Babylon.

"Bāb-ilim," I spoke softly to myself, "God's Gate. In Hebrew, Babel. In Arabic, Aṭlāl Bābil. This was the capital of southern Mesopotamia, from around 700 BC to 2000 BC."

I thought about the sheer magnificence of the city. By 700 BC, Babylon was at the height of its power. The largest city in the world at the time, spanning 10 square kilometers, it was the first city to have a population exceeding 200,000. It became the main commercial center of its region, drawing foreign conquerors due to its wealth and prestige. It was also a literary and religious center, dedicated to the worship of God Marduk.

"Imagine being born in Babylon!" I said aloud. "We are talking 2000 BC. Or being born in Vinča, another city of eternal fame. Both cities, cursed and blessed by so many, the best when at the height of their expression, scientifically supreme in many aspects... managing people, wealth, education, resources, benefiting ALL, including the generations of our time."

I let my mind wander, contemplating the symbols and ancient teachings that had shaped civilizations. The artistic images of the Universe, the secrets hidden in the development of language, told of three original principles, three gods, three sounds: the very foundation of the Platonic system of knowledge, or the Taoist explorations of ancient China.

"It was in ancient Serbia, ancient India, and ancient Malta, in Alexandria, that the Gnostics laid the foundation for this Neolithic, Taoist, Platonic trinity doctrine," I mused, the words carrying weight in my mind. "A Gnostic, a philosopher devoted to the contemplation of divine things,

"A thought cloud," I whispered to myself, "that comes and goes, leaving us in awe of the errors' clown who mocks the performer in an unknown language. When faced with inner or exterior void-ness, stuck in the orbit of contempt, nothing moves forward."

I shook my head, trying to clear my thoughts. I was so immersed in my own company that I didn't notice Tobby's miao from the front of our house. With a few minutes to kill, I descended the stairs and found her sitting behind the wheel of one of the parked vehicles. She was staring vacantly toward the building site opposite.

I was tempted to ignore her, to keep walking, but there was something serene about the silence that enveloped her. The mischievous grin tugged at the corner of my lips, and with a sigh, I let her inside.

And then it hit me. "Yes, the Tower of Babel..."

In the center of the town, there stood a great temple dedicated to God Marduk, called Esagila. A city and a temple full of stories. Of gods, of people, and of timeless wisdom.

The Hanging Gardens of Babylon, built around 600 BC, are one of the Seven Wonders of the World. Just to give you an idea of how the place looked: from the temple, the paved Processional Way passed by, its walls decorated with lions, bulls, and dragons. To the east of the Processional Way, private dwellings were built around central courtyards. Between the inner and outer defense walls lay irrigated land, connected by a network of canals. Greek philosophers referred to the Hanging Gardens of Babylon as the most beautiful man-made structure of the known world. The original Ishtar Gate of Babylon, once part of the city's grandeur, can now be seen on display at Berlin's Pergamon Museum, since 1930.

"So who built such an advanced city?" I pondered aloud, "Who were the Amorites?"

By around 2000 BC to 700 BC, much of southern Mesopotamia was occupied by the Amorites, a people who led a semi-nomadic lifestyle, herding sheep. To trace their presence, historians look to their language. They were Northwest Semitic speakers. The Amorites: pronounced /ˈæməˌraɪts/ are known by many names: Sumerian MAR.TU, Egyptian Amar, Hebrew אמורי (ʾĔmōrī), and in Ancient Greek, Ἀμορραῖοι.

"The Amorites established several prominent city-states in existing locations," I reflected. "The term Amurru in Sumerian texts refers both to them and to their principal deity."

The Amorites were among the first Semitic people whose language evolved into several of the languages we know today, including Arabic, Amharic, Tigrinya, Hebrew, Tigre, and Aramaic. In fact, Maltese, the language of my beloved Malta, is a direct descendant of these early Semitic tongues.

I paused, reflecting further. "The Phoenician alphabet, of which Maltese is a part, is one of the most important legacies of the Amorites. It served as the source for the Greek alphabet, and later the writing systems of Aramaic, Hebrew, and Arabic."

The Amorites were often depicted as nomadic tribes under chiefs, and they gradually pushed into lands where they could graze their herds.

Leaders with Amorite names assumed power in various places.

I continued, "The Amorite monarchs led revolutions of their time. They freed the citizens of several cities from taxes and forced labor. They also distributed royal land, creating a society of large farmers, free citizens, and enterprising merchants."

This shift had a profound impact on their economy. "Men, land, and cattle ceased to belong solely to the gods, temples, or the king," I mused. "Economic life was no longer in the hands of priests and kings."

The Amorites, as described in the Bible, were said to inhabit the land of Canaan. In Genesis 10:16, they are described as descendants of Canaan (Cain), powerful people of great stature, "like the height of the cedars" (Amos 2:9), often referred to as "giants."

"Giants," I repeated, as though the word itself held significance beyond mere myth. "Some even claim that the Amorites were a tribe of Aryan warriors. Can you imagine? Their size and strength, perhaps not so different from the Mediterranean Megaliths, the dolmens, and standing stones found across Syria, Lebanon, Iraq, and beyond."

Indeed, there is archaeological evidence that links these megalithic structures to giants. A semicircular arrangement of megaliths was even discovered at Atlit Yam, a site now submerged in the sea off the coast of Israel, dating back to 7,000 BC.

I couldn't help but connect this to the Megalithic Temples of Malta, which were constructed between 3600 BC and 2700 BC. "Locals in Malta call these temples the Temples of Giants," I said with a smile. "These ancient wonders are UNESCO World Heritage Sites and are among the oldest free-standing structures on Earth."

But all these ancient mysteries… what did they leave us?

Chamber after chamber, I navigated the maze, an experience that predated the Egyptian pyramids by a thousand years, and even more so, came five thousand years before the birth of Buddha or Christ.

At the very bottom of the Maltese Hypogeum complex, while meditating in the Oracle room, I could hear every whisper from the sound engineers seven meters above me. It was in this sacred place that I entered a profound meditation. The deep, resonating sounds of bells and ancient tribal instruments filled the air, while the ground beneath me vibrated at a frequency of 111Hz, a frequency that seemed to elevate the entire space and transcend the audience into higher states of consciousness.

On full moon nights, while meditating at Ġgantija, when the temples were unmarked by wires and pathways untouched by modern construction, the megalithic stones and the full moon took me into a similar VITRIOL experience. During these meditations, I could envision a young woman sleeping on the stone floor of the temple, connecting with her unborn child. I could see silhouettes of individuals dancing or chanting in prayer, absorbing healing energy, while others stood in quiet seclusion, invoking blessings.

Jerusalem, the spiritual center for Christians, Muslims, and Jews, is located between the Mediterranean and the Dead Sea. This sacred city has been the focal point for the three major monotheistic religions. Both Israel and the Palestinian Authority claim Jerusalem as their capital. Throughout its tumultuous history, the city has been destroyed, captured, and recaptured 44 times.

The Old City, which covers an area of just one square kilometer, houses the Temple Mount, the Dome of the Rock, al-Aqsa Mosque, and the Church of the Holy Sepulchre. In Islam, Jerusalem is considered the third holiest city, after Mecca and Medina, as it is the site of Muhammad's Night Journey.

If you live within Gaia's north you have implemented free health and education for all. This brings us to the statistic of 50% of people over 25 with the University degree in Russia that had a huge Government investment in human resources that is now paying off, or in Korea, in Switzerland, Germany or Scandinavia, the richest countries in Europe, around 50% of the University graduates in the US, and 35% in the UK that still supports the combination of Public and Private model of education.

If you are born anywhere in the poor South, you probably come from a rich family, like the Buddha, son of the King, or you truly believe in research, so you as Leonardo da Vinci or Pythagoras had done, made them a center of your life-long quest.

If you are in the Vatican State, you will know that just the Sistine Chapel in Rome has been visited yearly by 6 million visitors, the museum generates around $87 million from ticket revenue and another $30m from merchandising.

In sociology, we acknowledge the difference between the Eastern and Western personality types. Cultural rather than geographical divide, we mentally associate Asia with the East, and Australia, Europe, and America with the West. Some scholars would define Russia as East, and Islamic nations regard predominantly Christian nations as the West.

"The same stream of life that runs through my veins night and day runs through the world and dances in rhythmic measures. It is the same life that shoots in joy through the dust of the earth in numberless blades of grass and breaks into tumultuous waves of leaves and flowers. It is the same life that is rocked in the ocean-cradle of birth and of death, in ebb and in flow..."

Stream of Life, a Bengali poem by Rabindranath Tagore

Albert Einstein says

"I cannot prove scientifically that Truth must be conceived as a Truth that is valid independent of humanity; but I believe it firmly. I believe, for instance, that the Pythagorean theorem in geometry states something that is approximately true, independent of the existence of man."

If you are a woman sincerely practicing any system of knowledge, your inner most being would confirm that they were designed for men. The cultural revolution, that had happened a 100 years ago has liberated women, such a short time-span for asserting any claims or drawing any conclusions!

Baba-Ji was also referred to as: The King, the Guru, the Chosen One, or simply as Baba. There were no other Kings quite like him in the whole Kingdom of Humans living their Lilliputians lives all around him. Babaji had many wives, lovers and devas and they were all faithful followers of his life, message, and work.

Inside the hall of fame, within his living area, he hung portraits of Shiva, Buddha, Jesus, Baba Ji and one of himself in his 20s, and asked his devotees to daily sing praise to each of the images.

His message was simple: 'We are all love. Remember the time when you are truly in love, how happy and radiant you are!'

Know Thyself, and you'll know love. He exclaimed!

What a noble goal! What a noble man! What a noble fight! I've heard a whisper waking me from my hypnosis. The fight for truth always made a strong impression on me...

Back to Serbia, Dragan was his name, he walked through the woods surrounded by youth dressed in white robes woven with gold. Instructing the ladies to shower him with rose petals he walked slowly, appearing extraordinary large.

New John De-Baptist I am, announcing the second coming of Christ.

His sermon was on a field where he had improvised a river with a line of plastic crossing the field diagonally.

> This is the river Jordan, he dramatically stated, baptize, you, sinners!

Watching this scene in half horror, half amusement, jumping over the Jordan River left-right-left-right, followed by many disapproving eyes for ruining the sacredness of the place, I was only 20 at the time, but the mockery of the whole act was so blatantly evident! We were around 300 surrounding him, I wondered how could this possibly be legal...

It has all started and in its puzzling complexity ends with the worship of God (in Arabic the name for God is Alah) or divine, with its omnipresent Cosmic entity, in Taoism known as Tao, materialised through trinity of forces (in Hindhuism known as rajas, satwas and tamas) within four elements of Gaia: earth, water, sun, and air.

Many educated men crossed swords on this subject of use of magic within one's spiritual practices. While we acknowledge that lighting candles and burning sage (tamian) is beneficial, the sacredness of chanting is acknowledged all around the world, so where do we draw the line?

In Ethiopia, where Christianity is as ancient as 200 AC, I have experienced its Orthodox beauty with endless musical interactions and drumming on large instruments within the Addis Abeba Monastery. Singing names of God with Tibetan Buddhist while in Nepal with endless "Om Mani Padme Hum", was the same experience.

When in Lamu, in Kenia, I had a privilege to be a part of a Catholic worship ceremony. The Kenyans got out their musical instruments, singing Christ and Maria's chants. Needless to say, that I was the only white person in the crowds, in this standing collective prayer, that had lasted 2 hours. This is the mass, the Sunday celebration, I am now experiencing in Malta.

"It is difficult to fight for something that had never been in your hands", on an activists' meeting, a young environmentalist from Russia told the group: "in Malta the coastal areas were as a possession passed from the Knights to the British to the Developers for the use of the Rich."

During the medieval times of Serbia, we had used red-hot stones for cooking, just after milking sheep or goats, the milk would be poured in the hollowed pumpkin with the heated rocks inside. The vegetables were cooked in the same way. Heated stones were used for the preparation of skorup, or kaymak, white butter like cheese.

Porridges made from barley, oats and millet and broths with vegetables are still prepared in all the small mountain huts. Bread made from the mix of wheat, rye and barley, was a base of the diet of our ancestors, this is why we find some great baking skills within almost every family in Serbia.

During our past, meat was rarely eaten usually consumed during the festivals and the religious holiday.

During the first Serbian constitution, the Zakonopravilo, that dates back to 1219, and during Dušan's Empire, a century later, when Serbia vastly expanded over the Byzantine Empire, we were famous for building many Christian Ortodox Monasteries, had specialized in wine-making and bee-keeping passing the skill down to children for generations. The honey products and seasonally collected dried herbs are used across the country for healing of various diseases.

The hill of Soko Banja's (Serbia) 5th century Fortress rose sheer up from the plain. It was fortified by a large belt of rocks. Climbing up during the late hours each morning, we saw a dance of vapors of smoke ascending towards the sky forming the most amazing rainbows. I was told that the water of the well is sacred, and was never used accept for healing.

We were on our pilgrimage finding a water source at different times of the day, sometime at sunrise, or at sunset, gathering around the fire or water buzzing with bees and insects.

During my stay there, we ate no animal food, only oats, berries, and fruits of the season like the locals do.

All four of us had our hair long, dressed in simple cotton clothes like the old Macedonians; we walked barefoot through the mountains. We carried a wooden stick each, slowly moving through the meadows.

We crossed a plane before we met her, an old, wise woman, collecting all sorts of aromatic plants. Recognizing each other by sparks in our eyes, we kept each other company walking towards a water source exchanging healing crafts. She was initiating us into some of the secrets of the plants found in the valley or in the market.

"This is a very useful shrub, she handed what I knew to be cinnamon to me, so attractive to goats, that if you hold it in your hands they will follow you whining like babies and repelling to the ants, that if they smell it they will remove their nest from your home..."

Directly under the cliffs where the chamomile grows, cliffs that are un-accessible to men, a group of youths was climbing the neighboring trees collecting various fruits – plumbs, apples, pears. The butterflies observed this little ritual watching them from the distance, feasting on the sight of people tearing the clustered fruits from the bushes. Each morning when we passed, the trenches were full of new ripe berries, ready to be collected by passers-by with the sun-rise.

My memories of a mass sung in an Ethiopian Orthodox Christian Monastery is a memory of deep male voices and the sound of drums. My memory of a Tibetan Buddhist chant sung within the Monasteries of Tibet in Nepal where I spent a month learning about Tibetan Buddhism is the same deep continuous chanting of God's names. 11 meters deep within the Maltese Hypogeum, a 7,000 years old Sacred temple carved in stone, the Oracle Room where I prayed silently, resonated with 111Hz, altering states of Consciousness.

Do you get how powerful and spiritually strong this place is?

Within the Ancient Egyptian mythology, Isis creator god, her father, is Atum or Ra.

Isis was a major goddess within ancient Egypt, the time of our travel is 2500 BC, the area we are observing is the Ancient Egyptian and Greco Mediterranean worlds. Mother of Horus, and a wife to Osiris she was in charge of the mortals after death experiences, her image is linked to funerary practices and magical texts and temple rites of the pharaoh. Possessing healing powers, in art usually portrayed as a woman wearing a throne hieroglyph on her head.

In one myth, Isis creates a snake that bites Ra, and in an exchange for the cure, to extract the venom, Ra gives her the supreme secret of his true name - a sound that gives an ultimate power. She passes the name to Horus, her son. HRiS-T?

Many researchers explored Isis's name hoping to follow her through the ages. Her Egyptian name was ⬚st, or Ēse in the Coptic form of Egyptian, and ῏Ισις Isis in Ancient Greek.

The Pyramid Texts, 2400 BC, suggest the nature of the pharaoh to be both Horus and Osiris. The pharaoh as Horus in life becomes Osiris in death, where s/he unites with the other gods. New incarnations of Horus are blessed as new pharaohs. Isis is an etheric mum of Pharaohs, while an incarnated divine soul of her son Horus is within their material form on Earth. This is the reason why many of the oldest-known Egyptian pharaohs were only known by the name of Horus.

She was the goddess, energy, spirit that makes a man into a king. Her son Horus was an incarnate of each living pharaoh.

Greek and Egyptian culture were highly intermingled at this time, one could probably see the same rituals dedicated to Isis in Egyptian temples and in front of her statue inside a Greek temple.

In Egyptian mythology Horus was the god of light, often depicted as a man with the head of a falcon. Since Horus is the sky, his images have the sun as his right eye and the moon as his left.

Djet was the fourth pharaoh of the First Dynasty. Djet's Horus name means "Horus Cobra" or "Serpent of Horus".

Also known as the Golden Horus Name, this form of the pharaoh's name is the image of a Horus falcon perched above or beside the hieroglyph for gold.

Horus Falcon Bronze Statue 2600 BC in Brooklyn Museum

The symbol for "dragon" in Chinese is long 龍, also associated with good fortune, traditionally having power over rain. Many East Asian deities have dragons as their companions. The Emperor of China was the only one permitted to have dragons carved on his house, clothing, or personal articles.

The mušḫuššu is a Mesopotamian dragon with the body and neck of a snake, the front legs of a lion and the back legs of a bird.

The Ishtar Gate (Arabic: بوابة عشتار) of the city of Babylon was constructed in 575 BC by King Nebuchadnezzar II, and it is now in Berlin's Pergamon Museum. It was excavated in the early 20th century, and reconstructed using original bricks. The gate is decorated with mušḫuššu (dragons), aurochs (bulls), and lions, symbolizing the gods Marduk, Adad, and Ishtar. Covered in a blue glaze representing lapis lazuli, the gate, as a part of the Walls of Babylon.

The Ishtar Gate was only one small part of the city that had the palace, temples, an inner fortress, gardens, etc. of Babylon. The inscription of the Ishtar Gate is 2,600 years old and it is written in Akkadian cuneiform, 15 meters tall by 10 meters wide and includes 60 lines of writing, whereby King of Babylon tells us that: "...Marduk was seen as the divine champion of good against evil, and the incantations of the Babylonians often sought his protection."

In Babylonian astrology, Marduk was connected to the planet Jupiter.

Interestingly the Greek god Zeus is the Greek equivalent for Jupiter.

Stepping into Greek mythology, we now have the three brothers, Zeus, Hades and Poseidon. Zeus has thunder and is in charge of the Sky (Son, light), often seen as law and order; Hades has the magic kynee, an invisibility helmet that helps him rule the underworld (dreams, sub consciousness, death or after-death experiences) and Poseidon has the trident and rules the Sea. In Plato's Critias, the island of Atlantis was Poseidon's domain. Zeus is later often depicted as a bull.

Pythagoras who was well known in Magna Graecia and was a teacher of Plato, and Aristotle, around 530 BC, travelled to Croton, where he founded a spiritual school where initiates lived a communal, ascetic lifestyle, were vegetarians, studied philosophy, art, music, numbers, and discussed God.

Pythagoras gave the name of Monad (1) to God, and Dyad (2) to matter. The first and highest aspect of God is described by Plato as the One. The Monad (indescribable) emanated the Demiurge (Tao, Consciousness, Transcendent Source) or the creator. Plato, in the Socratic dialogue Timaeus, refers the Demiurge as a benevolent force that has created the world out of Chaos. Plotinus who is noted as the founder of Neoplatonism metaphorically identified the Demiurge as the Greek God Zeus.

Aristotle equated matter with the formation of the elements moved to action by force or motion. These two are known as Aristotle's Energeia and Plato's Demiurge.

The Demiurge of Neoplatonism is the Nous (mind of God), and it is:

1. Arche – "beginning" or the source of all things,
2. Logos – "reason" or the cause behind all,
3. Harmonia – "harmony" reflected with the Numbers in mathematics

It would seem then that the Orphic view of the Demiurge was integrated into Jewish and Christian Gnosticism. Later within the Judeo-Christian tradition the Demiurge or creator became Lucifer or Satan with the firmly attributed evil to the concept of Creation, whereby God wishes to limit man's knowledge by forbidding him the fruit of knowledge in paradise, while within the teachings of Pythagoras and Plato there is no "lesser", or "worse" God creating Universe and Humankind, even-though the Universe is in Chaos.

Schopenhauer in his Parerga and Paralipomena, published in 1851, wrote of this Neoplatonist philosopher: "With Plotinus there even appears, probably for the first time in Western philosophy, idealism that had long been current in the East even at that time, for it taught that the soul has made the world by stepping from eternity into time, * 'For there is for this universe no other place than the soul or mind'..."

Full moon on the Southern Gaia's Hemisphere came expectedly yet surprisingly different. She met Him in full force, face to face, keeping us, mortals, speechless, causing a mini Universal Chaos within the elements. So exciting was their pre-meditated and long awaited Cosmic dynamic Relief. Both a black cat and a black dog crossed my path this morning, reminding me to "remember" to stay awake and exchange with the souls I meet. Pausanias a Greek traveler of 200 AC, describing ancient Greece from his travels, says that Poseidon was one of the caretakers of the oracle at Delphi before Olympian Apollo took it over.

Malta, that could have been Atlantis, where now the ancient Temples stand for 5,000+ years, could have carried that "Oracle", with its Priests descending into the Hypogeum, 11 meters deep carved in stone underground Temples that even today resonate with sound perfectly, meditating entering into altered states of consciousness, into prayers and union with Divine, into dreams or Samadhi. conquered

Back in time, that has changed only a 150 years ago, pre-electricity, our society was infected with inequality, injustice, and a thought that lived within 99% of us for many millennia's - the thought of Equality. The total population of the world, post electricity, rose dramatically from 1/2 a billion to 8 billion. During this time of learning how to live together we went through both the 1st and the 2nd World War.

Thanks to the modern technology, we now have an opportunity to study / practice ancient spiritual growth / self-development practices from around the world. This exposure to the mix of East and West, South and North, offers inspiring insights.

A grand piano recital of one of the best world pianist Grigory Sokolov entitled "The Legend is Back" took us onto a 3 hours journey through

Haydn's sonatas finishing with 5 encores at midnight. While on this "single man on a piano" marathon, we, his audience, stopped breathing with every pause. He had mastered his and the energy of entire Conference Centre crowd, taking us into the highest states of consciousness.

Both music and sports, fully intuitively connect with the mastery of breath and souls' meditations. There is no exceptional artist, or sportsman or dancer without the mastery of deep breath, circular breath, rapid breath, or magic of concentration.

Within the spiritual growth arena, humanity has exercised tremendous efforts to transform Yin into Yang, searching for Balance within Chaos, at times applying force to guard "chastity", "honor", or "inner laws".

Within our understanding of the "wisdom" system, like in any learning, we pass through a spiral, climbing up its various levels – physically, mentally, intuitively mastering the tools, comprehending its more subtle wisdom. Exercising Tai Chi, for example, is a journey that combines breathing, movement, and the energy flow.

Watching a Master exercise the Art, we experience him / her exchange with Tao / divine.

Our ancestors' wisdom included applying a "personal growth" system to all age groups – kids, youth, mature adults, elderly.

Yoga, as a system of knowledge, went into many details of how energies within our spines interact with the brain, involving drawings (mandalas), sounds (mantras), symbols (within each of 7 chakra). Yoga practitioner examines how the various physical, mental or emotional dirt within the body creates emotional blockages.

Mastering concentration, meditation or breath, brings both: the prolonged life and enlightenment. Yoga "solder-like" practices had been designed for the improvement of Willpower. Practiced by mainly men, it was learned from the childhood. It had come from a predominantly Yin environment where the state of chaos is a norm, so it required discipline, as the male application of force. It assumed abstinence, the death of a practitioner came at the age of 39, so the time-span of temptations and the strength / ability of practice were very different.

Both Yoga and Tai Chi, products of Yin based minds, are meant to be practiced alone. Children because of their Yang nature are less attracted to these exercise systems.

The western sports were designed with the competitiveness and the social aspect in mind, both products of predominantly Yang based minds. Applying the western exercise to various age groups, we get the regular nature walks, mountaineering, etc.

A tennis player has to play a 6 hours within a typical tournament. If he does not have an inner strength to perfect his/her breath there is no possibility of success. Following the same knowledge, a Serbian top tennis player, Djoković, moved his diet into a vegetarian, gluten free one and later in his life into a raw vegan one, gaining benefits from the consumption of "live" foods. From a Yang based culture, in today's world meat dominated diet, the ancient Yin knowledge has been hidden within the practices of Monks, and long periods of Orthodox Christian fasts, or remembered as the natural vow of austerity practiced amongst the poor.

When my mum died of Alzheimer I had a hard time deciding what to do with all my good old never to be listened to again LPs, all the classics within the family library, but my Russian Worker was stolen before I even contemplated its destiny. Its mystical disappearance when I departed my home-land in a search for better future gave this first icon a romantic always to be remembered overtone.

Luxury was never something we knew, yet we travelled twice a year to places rich in culture and history: Vienna, Rome, Istanbul, and Athens throughout my childhood. My father lost both his parents when he was just 18. Left with four siblings, no money, and no relatives to rely on, he nevertheless completed his PhD in Law and went on to publish an impressive 27 legal books. At home, we spoke often of Utopia and Plato, analysing Roman Law and its flaws, discussing Tolstoy's sense of social justice, and seeking a perfect social system. Conversations about our inner drive towards perfection were as integral to my upbringing as the breast milk that nourished me during my early years.

Through reading the works of Russian and Greek philosophers, I was introduced to the ideals of equality, social and economic justice, and a world where true democracy prevailed — where workers held power, education and healthcare were free for all, and monopolies did not exist. With my father's lectures on Co-operative Law, his dream became mine.

When I was 16, I discovered meditation, and it marked the beginning of a new path. Hermann Hesse's The Glass Bead Game opened my eyes to a new world of spiritual and intellectual discovery. Without the need for alcohol, drugs, or medication, I embraced the life of a yogi. A monk without a monastery, deeply connected to ancient spiritual practices, I would chant mantras, light candles, and drum in sacred circles.

The collapse of Yugoslavia and the bankruptcy of its banks arrived in our lives just as my father's diabetes—insulin-dependent for 15 years—began to take its toll. His kidneys failed, his sight was lost, and his body became covered in sores caused by vitamin imbalances, a common complication of dialysis. His lungs filled with water, causing a relentless cough. By this point, my mother had suffered her first nervous breakdown, later diagnosed with Alzheimer's. Becoming her caregiver was a daunting task, as I was also studying Economics. Yet it taught me much about the strengths and weaknesses of Western medicine, particularly when it came to healing.

Watching my father fade away was heartbreaking. Equally devastating was witnessing the collapse of my country. I will never forget waiting outside a pharmacy for five hours just to get my father's regular bottle of insulin. Five hours, can you imagine? For something so basic, so necessary.

Do we truly need suffering to grow?

In those difficult times, I found solace in Mika, our housekeeper, babysitter, and cook, who stayed with us for seven years. She had only one book: a large dictionary of Serbian Folk Magic (Veliki Narodni Sanovnik) and at the age of five, I was introduced to its secrets. Through Mika, I learned about magic, palmistry, fortune-telling, dream interpretation, coffee cup readings, and the oracle of beans for divination. The mystical world of Serbian Gypsy folk magic became a part of my life.

My father would often say that Mika never knew how to lie. Born in a village near Belgrade, she would save every penny of her salary to send to her brother. She limped, her foot crippled by a bullet, a wound she said was inflicted by a man from her village. My father suspected this was her only lie, a carefully guarded secret to protect her ex-husband, a man we never met. He was likely an abuser and a drunkard, someone she refused to speak of. He stayed with their newborn child, who tragically died soon after Mika left him.

Despite her own painful past, Mika's gentle and humble nature postponed my own fears and nightmares. When my mother's anxieties manifested as monstrous, fiery dragons or warriors, Mika's presence softened the terror I might have otherwise felt.

My mother, misunderstood by her own family, had come from a background of hardship. Her father had once owned horses before the war, and during the Second World War, he had taken in refugees and lost much of his property to the communists. My grandmother later worked as a shop assistant in the same bakery. My grandfather, like many men of his time, saw little value in educating a woman, believing she would marry and that her education would be unnecessary. As a result, my mother completed only one year of higher education while working.

Her struggle was emblematic of the generation of women trying to prove their equality while raising a family. She couldn't bear the long hours of teaching while also managing a family with two chronically ill members.

As she tried to navigate her role as a mother and wife, my mother resorted to physical punishment. Our backs were often bruised from her hands, leather belts, or coat hangers. The discipline she had been taught manifested in us, and as we grew older, the tension in the household mounted. One year after Mika's departure, my father, too weak to act, finally filed for divorce. Our home became a battleground of constant arguments, and my memories of it are coloured with bitterness.

Though I was only six, my parents made me my sister's special needs assistant. It was an impossible role for a child, but it was the reality we faced. Our teenage years were defined by bullying, which we both endured relentlessly.

I don't know if you've ever encountered the Mythical Mare, that figure from our subconscious that visits children in the form of nightmares. But for me, she came every night, tormenting me until I learned how to fly in my dreams. I struggled with the idea of "It is never too late to relive your childhood happily", because for me, those words had never been married to reality.

The fairies of inner alchemy did not always protect us. My parents were so caught up in their own Shadow Work that they failed to see the depth of the trauma we were enduring.

My sister spent two years of her childhood in and out of hospitals, undergoing hip surgery, and she became terrified of doctors. The bullies at school found this amusing, chasing her with surgical needles and laughing at her screams. No one intervened. No one helped.

This memory never fades, I was the silent witness, the one who knew what was happening, even as my sister buried it deep in her subconscious. Only I remember.

In my early twenties, I spent five years caring for my father. I cleaned his wounds, helped him walk, read, eat, and move. Often, I found them locked in a battle of words that would leave my father in a diabetic coma and my mother in a senseless state. The ambulance would arrive to inject them both with insulin.

When it came time to choose a college, my parents disregarded my dream of studying archaeology and enrolled me in an administrative school instead, so I could help my sister finish her secondary education. Abandoning my passion for philosophy and archaeology was painful, but I did it. At 18, overwhelmed and lost, I contemplated ending my life.

But in that darkness, I discovered meditation...

When I entered the world of parenting, adopting two giggly bundles of joy, my life's focus shifted entirely. It was fascinating how the subconscious patterns that formed the foundation of my relationships extended into the world of parenting. The dynamics of love, growth, and connection began to unfold in vibrant hues I never imagined. It felt like a magnified view of humanity's heartbeat, and it was beautiful.

In Belgrade, my birthplace, people accepted my children with such warmth, as if they were marvels from another world. "Can I photograph her?" asked the woman at Grinet, a charming coffee shop that opened in 1991, just as I was beginning my journeys outside of Serbia. It was a place I had discovered before leaving in April 1993, with its delicate flower-patterned wallpaper and handpicked coffees from across the globe. Its Mokachino — a delightful fusion of coffee, froth, and chocolate — was legendary. The woman knelt to Ema's level, laughing with her, as they shared a spontaneous photo session.

"A cookie for you," said the baker from Aca Baker, my childhood bakery down the street. The pastries there — biscuits, bagels, rolls, muffins, cakes, cookies — were still the best in town. "It has strawberries. She can eat strawberries, can she?" asked the lady, kneeling behind the counter to give her a hug.

"Can I touch her hair?" asked a boy waiting for a bus near the Youth Centre. Another stranger, a shop assistant in an Indian souvenir shop, exclaimed, "How beautiful you are!" and presented a gift for both my daughter and me, insisting we take them without payment.

It was like stepping into a world where love and kindness were abundant, simply because I was walking with my children. People saw us and saw something more — stories, shared destinies. I had stopped telling strangers that I had adopted my children, because every time I did, their reactions were so deeply emotional—some cried, others shared their own stories of fate.

In a park in Tashmajdan, a pensioner once told me, "I won't take my medicine today; I just had my medicine looking at you!" A twelve-year-old girl handed Ema a balloon, stepping back to watch her delight.

One day, in a macrobiotic health shop, a graceful teenage girl approached me with a tear in her eye. "My father is from Ethiopia," she confided. "He had to go back to Africa, leaving my mother pregnant in Belgrade. I never met him, and I don't speak Amaric... but seeing your daughter, I feel connected to my father's land. She is full of wonder."

Ema carefully examined her new elephant toy, listening intently. The shop owner smiled warmly, opening the door as we left, "Do you live nearby? I hope to see you again soon."

Every interaction, whether at a bookstore or with a street vendor, revealed a world that opened its arms to my children, and in return, they filled hearts with joy. As I watched Ema, so tiny at just 104 cm and 15 kg, a light within her seemed to connect all of us. She would giggle in a taxi, knock gently on the driver's shoulders, and ask him to honk, sending kisses to everyone in sight. "Bi-bip!" she would say, her joy contagious.

What fascinated me most about her, I often wondered, was her completely conscious eyes—so rare in a child her age—or was it her courage? A child from Ethiopia, taken from her homeland and placed in the arms of a Serbian mother. And yet, she thrived, her spirit unbroken. How did she carry such resilience, such openness?

I remember the first time I prepared her wardrobe, waiting eagerly for her arrival. I filled it with dresses in shades of pink, violet, and blue, waiting for her to grow into them — waiting for her to twirl and sing and become the princess and ballet dancer I imagined.

There was a divine spark in the moment of adoption. It came to me during a spiritual concert, in a deep meditation where celestial sounds guided me. The message came not in words, but in a profound knowing: "Now is the time to adopt." It felt less like a decision and more like an instruction, as if the Universe itself had whispered to me, confirming that this was my path.

By the time I celebrated my 40th birthday as a single woman, I knew this was my journey — one that didn't come with expectations of building a family in the traditional sense. No fertility anxiety or fears of biological differences clouded my mind. I knew my children were out there in the world, waiting for me to find them.

And so I did.

In exactly nine months, from the conception of the idea to the moment I held my children in my arms, I embarked on a deeply spiritual pregnancy. Each step of the adoption process felt effortless, as if I were moving in perfect harmony with the divine flow.

Though there were obstacles — misconceptions — every challenge only strengthened my resolve. "You must be crazy!" they said. "Why would you disrupt your perfect life to raise children as a single mother?" But inner whispers were louder than any of the voices. I knew this was my path.

And here they are now: Ema and her brother, two beautiful souls found their place in my heart, in my world. Together, we walk this path, guided by the wisdom of a Universe that always knew the way.

I've never had worries about growing old on my-own, I loved my Life, my 'perfect' spiritual bell. It is not my 'loneliness' that shaped my decisions. Perhaps because I had a chance to experience IT all, the great career, amazing travels, most enriching love life, deepest meditations, devoted friends & family, living in different countries, I had such a strong Soul-Urge to experience Motherhood and Mothering as a Spiritual Experience.

No Life Journey is an easy one, no lessons wasted in vain, during my 9 months of preparation or expectation I hit many invented 'No's: 'you are a foreigner in the lands you live in – the procedure must be very different', 'you are single – that is legally very different', 'you have no family in the lands you live in' (they knew not of my Universal Spiritual Family that was always with me) so I've learned to keep my questions for the informed ones or the ones who have already adopted and the world before my eyes changed into a reasonable procedure that is manageable and doable from all sort of perspectives.

Just before the 'fatal' Moment of Knowledge that I wish to enter the World of Motherhood adopting my lovely babies as a single mother I was involved in helping Father George, this amazing Franciscan Maltese Priest build one of his orphanages in a remote village in the outskirts of Ethiopia. He was the one to lead my re-Search into this most amazing of African countries and into an orphanage led by his dear friend Sister Ludgarda into the heart of Addis Abeba, Ethiopia. Experiencing this country for the first time I wrote:

> I've never seen so much poverty, so much elegance, so much beauty. Such gracious walks, so many warm & responsive eyes. So many blind & deaf, so much dust. So many perfect hair-styles. Such wonderful climate. So little bushes and trees. So many people walking Beside each other Hugging & holding hands. So many people dying of AIDS. So many heads turning towards the church - praying. So many perfectly white shirts. So few old people. So many people with crutches. So many hands greeting each other. Such thin cats and friendly babies. Like in Ethiopia...

i went to the cradle of civilisation
to see the root of problems
of human selfishness and un-consciousness

i went to the bottom to understand the peak
facing death, starvation, disease
i was surrounded with kindness, love and peace
Is this the Rule?

In the elevator of my office building, I had mentioned to Father George that I wished to adopt.

"I help an orphanage in Addis," he said with a gentle smile, his eyes full of warmth. "And 'combinazioni,' Sister Ludgarda, who runs the orphanage, is here in Malta visiting for a few days. Let me call her, and we can have lunch together. Today?"

Father George was a man of action, and everything for him seemed to happen in the now. No delays, no waiting. His energy was contagious, and I could feel a sense of urgency building within me.

"Today?" I repeated, surprised but grateful.

"Yes, today," he nodded with certainty, already pulling out his phone to call her. "This is how things get done."

So, just like that, I met Sister Ludgarda during her week-long visit to Malta. I couldn't believe the timing. What a coincidence!

A few months later when we spoke on the phone, I smiled nervously, trying to steady my racing heart. "I already bought the tickets," I said, eager to get things moving. "I will come to take the kids' blood for the lab check to Malta, and I'll bring the blessed chalices Father George sent for the new Church."

Sister Ludgarda listened closely, her voice reflecting understanding. She spoke in agreement. "Yes, we'll do that. we'll see each other soon."

Her approval was a sign that things were starting to fall into place. That tiny gesture had accelerated the adoption process — helping not only me but also three other adoptive couples and six children who had been waiting in the adoption queue. Even better, it reduced the cost for everyone involved. I would be acting as their paid nurse, carrying the blood samples for the health check-up from Ethiopia to Malta.

The best part for me? It meant that I would meet my kids before adopting them. It was a small step, but it felt like the first tangible connection, the first moment of something real taking shape in my heart.

The day after my 1st and 2nd arrival to Addis I gave endless gifts to the kids of the orphanage. We became friends very quickly. To the younger ones I bought jewelry, to the older ones I gave shoes, all behind Sister Ludgarda's back. Or so I thought, until Sister Ludgarda shared with me a story from 40 years ago, when she first started the orphanage.

"The first project I was involved in," she said with a gentle smile, "was buying shoes for the children."

Her kindness and humility made my heart swell. This beautiful woman, who had dedicated her life to the children in her care, had given me a full day to wander around the orphanage, soaking in the place, feeling the warmth of the atmosphere she had helped create.

The next day, as we sat together, she told me, "Tomorrow, you will need to decide, and we will get the documents ready for your baby."

Something stirred in me, and I asked, "What about adopting two instead of one child?"

Sister Ludgarda didn't hesitate. She simply smiled and said, "Let's see what we can do."

We exchanged a few emails with the Social Services Department, and by the next day, the answer came through: yes, as long as you have the Adoption Certificate, you can adopt as many as six children.

I could hardly believe it. Visiting the Kinder Mehret for the first time in November 2007, I went there with plans for one child, but I ended up falling in love with two. So, when I returned in February 2008, I came home with a larger family than I had originally planned.

I had gone to meet my baby girl and came back with my baby boy, Andrej, a three-month-old boy born just before I arrived at the orphanage, and Ema, a three-year-old girl who had arrived at the same time I did.

I remember noticing her in the middle of the room, surrounded by other children, her braids neatly done. And then I looked into her eyes — conscious, wise eyes. In that moment, I knew my life had changed forever.

I wrote:I stopped to ask you - your name

> it wasn't written on your forehead
> I stopped to enquire where you came from
> even though I saw a tag on your bracelet
> saying - Earth's womb
> I was intrigued by your voice
> and love that was pouring
> from your eyes
> I knew you - before I met you
> we laughed in my dreams
> many many years ago

Andrej has the most amazing hands: long fingers, and on his right palm, a sign of luck. He was the smallest baby in a room full of babies: 20, 30 of them, all sleeping together, cared for by 4 or 5 workers.

Visiting the baby room became a part of my daily routine. Each morning, I would spend 2 to 3 hours holding the babies, one by one, hugging them, whispering secrets to them. Sister Ludgarda had also assigned a few volunteers from Holland to stay with the babies, tasked with cuddling them each day, ensuring they felt loved and comforted.

Andrej was born in the orphanage. His mother had suffered a stroke that paralyzed her left side, and so she gave birth to him there, so that we could care for him.

"Three months old," Sister Ludgarda told me one day, her voice gentle yet matter-of-fact. "That is the reason why he is not yet on the list to be adopted. We usually wait until a baby is six months old to make sure their motor skills are developing properly. But if you wish, he could be yours."

Taking the blood samples of six kids across three borders, Ethiopian, Italian, and Maltese, was a process full of paperwork and explanations, especially in Italian. But what stood out more than anything was the connection I felt to the children's souls as I carried their samples.

A flight from Africa to Europe with a suitcase full of blood samples, wrapped in tissue, was nothing short of mystical. I felt a deep connection to each child, almost as if I was part of their first journey into a new life.

When I arrived at the airport, there were three Maltese couples waiting for me, holding huge bouquets of flowers. "Welcome," read the sign they held in their hands. I had no idea I would be greeted with such warmth and excitement, yet here I was, carrying the blood of their soon-to-be children, the first photos of these little souls waiting for their arrival in just a few months. We all cried.

In January 2008, we got the green light to travel again: to Ethiopia to collect our children and finalize the legal procedure. I was one of three families traveling to Addis to bring six kids home.

We were given rooms with toilets, and the kids were handed to us almost immediately, though the official paperwork would take a month to finalize.

Connected by the same intentions and an abundance of goodwill, two families quickly became the best of friends. We decided to share our cooking, our time, and our lives, spending our days together in the visitors' quarters within the orphanage.

Having shared flats with other students in the past and experienced life in an ashram, I kept my distance. I cooked my own food and maintained my own routine. It wasn't until the third week that I had truly gotten to know the other parents. By then, we had forged strong, meaningful relationships.

Visiting Addis for the second time, I wrote:

i asked somebody what to bring to the orphanage in Africa
and the answer was - don't bring presents
you can not buy present for 150 children and
if you bring a present to one, the others will feel left out
so I went out and bought presents for 150 children
if they are not my ticket to heaven one day
they will become exploding drops of happiness

Children now know me by name and they run to greet me - now they feel that they can connect with me even further - I said I am coming back and I kept my word... :)

I bought them their first shampoo and gave them their first presents and they know that there is more and they give me that look of 'secret knowing'. I sit amongst them and they change my hair style in 10 minutes, they sit in my lap and play with my scarf, the small ones want to be held. We share secrets - Sisters do not know about them - I buy them lip-gloss that they are not allowed to wear and give them bracelets that they love... The orphanage is full of beautiful stories... Today I also saw their 3 cows and 10 chickens and I spoke to them too :)

In Addis even a begger moves through life ellegantlly. In the middle of the street noises, he sits as a sadhu, streight, proud, slow, untouched by any movement.

Very beautiful people walking pass me, I realised the sad hard core statistic of this place, around 60% of people are less than 16 years old.

Ethiopians still die young, before they are 40.

While in the Western worlds we see sickness in the old age people, in Ethiopia many get sick young, are on crouches, or get blind (not quite sure why). Apparently there is a lot of HIV. Since there is no Public Health even a small injury can lead to the fatal one. There is a Hospital in Addis, two young German volonteers went to visit, in an attempt to help, and came back to the orphanage crying and womitting. I dare not think what kind of sceens they have witnessed. Four in ten people within Ethiopia do not have clean water. It is puzzling how did we (Humanity) let this happen, so I researched the History books to find out what did really happen...

Around the 7th century BC, the kingdom of D'amt was established in northern Ethiopia with its capital Yeha. In the 5th century BC, the area was known as the Aksumite Kingdom. The Persian writer Mani listed Aksum with Rome, Persia, and China as one of the four great powers of his time. It was in the early 4th century AC that a Syro-Greek named Frumentius, converted King Ezana to Christianity, making Ethiopia one of the first countries with Christianity as the official state religion. He was given the title "Abba Selama" – a Father of Peace. It was around 1000 AC when the famous rock-hewn churches of Lalibela were carved.

This time was known as the period of peace and stability. Around 1270, the Solomonic dynasty came to rule Ethiopia. They claimed that they are direct descent from Solomon and the queen of Sheba who were the Kings of the Aksumite Kingdom.

In 1624, Jesuit missionaries converted the Emperor Susenyos to Roman Catholicism and this resulted in years of revolt and civil unrest and thousands of deaths. In 1632 Susenyos' son, Emperor Fasilides, declared the state religion to again be Ethiopian Orthodox Christianity, and expelled the Jesuit missionaries responsible for this unrest. All of this contributed to Ethiopia's isolation during the 17th and 18th century.

The 1880s were marked by the Italians who together with the British fought to influence the region. An Italian company bought a port Asseb, from the local Afar sultan, vassal to the Ethiopian Emperor, which by 1890 led to the formation of the Italian colony of Eritrea. Conflicts between the two countries resulted in a war in 1896, where the Ethiopians defeated the Italian forces and remained independent. It feels as though the Ethiopian independence somehow bordered the Colonial forces so they left it Be, during the 20th century progress, in a way isolated and incapable to exist within the existing economic order.

Ethiopia takes care of our coffee beans that we so readily worship yet it probably gets only a tiny percentage from the sale of this magic powder. The money is shared by Swiss and Italian monopolies who buy the coffee at ridiculous small prices and sell it to us, end users, deeply exploiting the system called Free Market Economy.

Many people I met and saw on the streets of Addis had HIV/AIDS. The majority of people dying from a disease (72%) died without any health treatment, at their homes not knowing or refusing to admit they have AIDS.

In Addis Ababa, there are 12 registered public hospitals, and it's the patients with non-communicable diseases like cancer who are most likely to die. Lung disease and cold have become commonly known terms synonymous with AIDS in the community. AIDS is a new disease, and while people still die from tuberculosis or a simple cold, the true culprit is often the virus, which destroys the immune system. Hard statistics estimate that around 36.7 million people worldwide are living with HIV/AIDS, and among them, 1.8 million are children born to infected mothers. Alarmingly, about 40% of these individuals— approximately 14 million—are unaware that they are infected.

Dinkinesh, a 60-year-old grandmother in Addis, lives with her six-year-old grandson, Brook. Her only daughter died of AIDS, following the death of her husband from the same disease, leaving behind four children. Sadly, this is not an isolated story. Sister Ludgarda runs a special room within the orphanage for children of all ages who are HIV-positive.

In the 1980s, we heard about various pop stars who were infected by the disease, and by the 1990s, HIV began spreading rapidly through Africa. This raised many questions—how could a virus that initially started in the West have spread to Africa? Could it be that heroin addicts from places like Lamu brought it to Sub-Saharan Africa?

I remember the first night after we became a family, on the 8th of February, 2008. It was a moment of universal experience for any parent. My diary entry reads:

> "From yesterday, I am a mum!!! I had my first nappy change, did it wrong, of course :)and my first bottle mixing (what do you put first, milk or water??!!). My first night without sleep (and the second one too, so I've decided to take on the Tibetan Buddhist practice of meditation during the night: wakeful sleep :) Million is helping me with chanting om-mani-padme-hum-aaaaaaaa-aaaaaaaa). And my first bath (Million was crying as though I was going to kill him) haha — we make a really good team :)"

However, just three days after we entered our new home as a family, we were robbed. All our precious belongings were stolen — technology, gold, and even sentimental items belonging to my father. We were asleep upstairs as the robbery took place in the middle of the night. When we had recovered and gathered some of our belongings back, the robbers returned to steal everything again.

Shortly after the adoption, my life took an unexpected turn. The reality of being a new mother to two young children, combined with the challenges at home, changed everything. My career, once a prominent and fast-paced part of my life, was no longer feasible. I was made redundant from my high-executive position. The company had been expanding, and my role involved frequent travel to the Netherlands and the UK to market our IT products. But now, with two young children and a mother who had developed Alzheimer's, it became clear that I could no longer juggle both.

I was barely through my morning routine when the email arrived, the words still echoing in my head:

"Dear Nataša,

After a thorough review of our staffing needs, we have made the difficult decision to restructure the team. As a result, we regret to inform you that your position, along with those of the marketing and PR department, is being made redundant. We appreciate the work you've done and wish you all the best in the future.

Sincerely,

Richard

I blinked, rereading the email, trying to digest the news. A wave of dizziness washed over me, not only from the suddenness of it all but also from the persistent, wheezing cough that had been nagging at me for weeks. Chronic bronchitis had crept into my life slowly but surely, and now it seemed like every breath felt like a battle.

I rubbed my chest and let out a soft cough, which turned into a harsh hacking sound. It had become a constant companion, never fully letting go. Even as I processed the news, I couldn't help but pause to catch my breath. My body felt like it was on the edge of collapse, yet I couldn't afford to stop.

With a deep sigh, I closed my laptop, swallowing the frustration that had begun to rise. The children needed me, and there was no time to waste feeling sorry for myself.

I stood up, forcing myself to ignore the coughing fit that followed, and walked into the living room where Andrej and Ema were playing.

"Good morning, my loves," I said, my voice coming out hoarse and strained from the coughing. I had learned to hide the fatigue and weariness from the kids, but the truth was I felt utterly drained.

Andrej, still just a baby, flashed me a sleepy smile from his crib, his tiny hands reaching toward me. Ema, now a bit older, was sitting on the floor, arranging her dolls in a circle.

"Mummy, I made a party for my dolls!" she exclaimed, holding up a tiny plastic cup. "You can come to my party later."

"That sounds wonderful, darling," I said, smiling despite the pain in my chest. I forced myself to sit down next to her and picked up one of the dolls, pretending to take part in the tea party.

As I did, another cough racked my body. I put a hand over my mouth, but it didn't help much, and the sound echoed through the room.

Later that day, as I tried to focus on daily tasks, I could feel the weight of everything bearing down on me. I had lost my career, my sense of control over my life, and now my body was betraying me. The coughing made it difficult to focus, and the pressure in my chest was almost unbearable.

That evening, after the kids were finally asleep, I sat on the couch, exhausted beyond measure. A light cough escaped from my chest, and I winced at the sound.

I leaned back into the cushions, letting my head rest, and for a moment, I allowed myself to simply feel the exhaustion. The demands of being a single mother, of taking care of two young children while also managing the needs of my mother with Alzheimer's, were weighing on me heavily. But I had no choice but to keep going.

I pulled my knees to my chest and closed my eyes, inhaling deeply— trying to find some peace in the chaos.

I could hear the soft rhythmic sound of Andrej's breath from the other room, and I smiled faintly. These moments, even the hard ones, were mine, and they were precious.

But when I coughed again, I knew I had to do something. I couldn't let the illness win, not when I had so much to give.

Three years later, I still remember the small victories. The first time I went to the bathroom alone. It wasn't a grand moment, but for me, it was a small slice of freedom in the midst of my overwhelming new reality.

I stood in the bathroom, the door shut and locked behind me, feeling the weight of the day lift for just a few moments. For the first time in a long while, I was alone with my thoughts.

When I walked out, Ema was sitting on the stairs, waiting for me with her little stuffed animal.

And with that, life moved forward. I had no choice but to keep going, to keep smiling, and to take care of the little ones who depended on me. Every day was a challenge, but there was no room to quit.

Now, I found myself facing a new and overwhelming reality. I had two young children to feed, and a mountain of financial obligations to meet.

The bank loan for the house, along with a recently purchased car, was hanging over me like an unrelenting storm cloud. I had hoped the car would help ease some of the financial pressure, but things quickly spiraled out of control. The government had just removed the import tax on second-hand cars, causing the market to crash. The car, which had cost me a significant amount, was now worth half of what I had paid for it, leaving me with no way to sell it for enough to repay the loan.

The weight of it all felt suffocating. On top of that, I was still a Serbian living in Malta, and as a foreigner, I wasn't entitled to any financial help from the government. I had hoped for a safety net, but I was quickly stripped of my savings.

There were days when I couldn't help but feel completely alone in this foreign land.

I remember one particularly quiet evening, sitting on the edge of my bed, the dim light from the lamp casting long shadows across the room. Ema and Andrej were asleep, their small breaths rising and falling in rhythm. I sat there, my mind racing, staring at the walls, as the ticking of the clock seemed to grow louder.

I held my head in my hands. "What do I do now?" I whispered to myself, my voice trembling.

Suddenly, the phone rang. It was my sister, calling from Serbia.

"Are you okay?" she asked, her voice concerned. "How are the kids? How are you holding up?"

Tears welled up in my eyes as I heard the familiar, comforting sound of her voice.

"I don't know, Manika," I replied, my voice shaky. "I feel like I'm drowning. I don't have enough to cover everything. No one's here to help me, and I don't even know where to turn."

"I wish I could be there," she said, her voice filled with regret. "But Mum… You know I have to stay with her. Her Alzheimer's is getting worse. She's not doing well at all."

"I know," I replied, trying to steady my breath. "I just… I just wish I could be there to help you with her..."

I could no longer meditate for hours like I used to, lost in the stillness of my thoughts, for the house was always filled with noise. The rhythm of my life had shifted, and with it, the quiet solitude of my meditation cave faded into the background of the everyday joys and worries of parenting. I had exited that peaceful sanctuary to embrace the whirlwind of raising two beautiful children.

But in the midst of it all, I held tight to one thing: my sacred space for meditation. It had simply shifted. I now found my moments of stillness in the very early hours of the morning, before the world awoke, or during the rare moments when I could put the babies to sleep, their tiny bodies nestled with me in the same bed.

"Shhh, it's time to sleep, my little ones," I would whisper softly, tucking them in and then retreating into a space of quiet reflection.

During these small pockets of time, I reminded myself of the principles I had chosen for this journey of motherhood. Inspired by the philosophy of Simplicity Parenting, I created a home filled with connection and presence. No gadgets, no distractions — just the pure, unfiltered bond between us.

As I held my babies close, I learned to trust their wisdom, following their cues, allowing them to lead me. Their innocent eyes, their tender laughter, their tears — all of it was a language I had come to understand deeply.

"I trust you, I trust us," I would silently say to them in my heart. "This is our journey together."

Through it all, I committed myself to the basic principle: I wish to live love and consciousness within this Parenting Journey, returning to this intention each day, over and over again. Every moment, every breath, was a choice to stay present, to cultivate love and awareness. It wasn't always easy, but it was always worth it.

I stayed attentive to the Whispers of the Soul, the gentle nudges that came when I needed guidance, when I needed to listen. I respected Gaia, the Earth, and all her creatures, understanding the deep interconnectedness that binds us all.

"Thank you, Mother Earth," I would often whisper while walking in nature, holding Ema's hand as she skipped beside me, Andrej tucked snugly in my blouse. "Thank you for supporting us."

The spectrum of emotional and mental states that came with this journey — the ups and the downs, the joy and the frustration — became part of the process. I embraced the challenge of transforming the crude into the subtle, refining my thoughts, my actions, my responses. I was learning, always learning.

In every small gesture, in every moment with my children, I found myself giving thanks to the Alchemy of the Soul. The simple act of being present with them became an alchemical process in itself. I could feel the shift as my soul was both shaped and shaped by theirs.

I realized that this was not just a journey of motherhood; it was the Alchemy of Humanity. Every thought, every action, every choice mattered — within the Matrix of Collective Knowledge. Every moment with my children became a building block, contributing to the greater good of all. The lessons they taught me were not just for me but for the world.

And in those quiet moments before dawn, when I would meditate, I would think about all the lives we touch, all the lives our actions ripple through. Every action is done for the Benefit of All.

"I'm doing this for us," I whispered, to the universe, to the children. "For the world. For love." A prayer I noted in my Soul's Diary just after the adoption:

> Please re-create me again! Let me go behind beyond when my Soul dares to imitate God and breaks the mortal edge of restrictions, boundaries, pre-programmed codes, prejudices and un-written laws. Let me bind my limbs with blind-fold of love, burn disappearing in the light of inspiration, go through walls chanting mantras of compassion, laugh screaming-off the last remains of air, walk surrounded by the shiniest beings ever lived on this plane. Re-create me, I know you can!

Awakening

I woke up with a thought - do you remember?

A feather or
a tickle at the bottom of the pond of memories
buried a sound...

Opening my eyes, I whispered - is this a mistake?

An error on the page kept bouncing back
could not handle the failure of its own reflection

I let them come-in and stayed puzzled with the mad noises - madness?

In an instant 100s of faces crammed within the same story
Move away - I shrugged them off
I need some air!

I looked around and found nothing but zero trying to become zero-ness

Wall covered with golden leafs
stopped me on the way to Hell
I peeled them off one by one
discovering layers of nothingness
filled with space and the sound of AUM

When I for the first time have publicly recited this poem on a gathering of poets in Cambridge, my voice trembling, hands shivering and a French girl somewhere in the middle of the audience cried.

Why are we here?

'I will show you fear
In a handful of dust...'

& passion & fire & desire
and no, no, no
we will not give up at once
& it will feel as it is the first time
every time
& we will punt & scream & sight
& swear FOREVER, NEVER
in line with the rules & always for the first time

Something amazing has happened! But maybe it hasn't...

You offer life and drops of water
That carry within its heart the desire to experience
The spring
With the fear of the in-evitability of its end

And how unreal and absurd our passion is
When deprived of the context of T I M E
And how strange our struggle is
When deprived of the frame of M I N D

Jump into the whirlpool and discover me
In the 16th century as a mistress of a Count
At the very beginning as Eve
And now at the bank of Cam
Waiting for a bridge to be built.

Who do you believe you are?
A goddess, a student or a tramp
A word lost in translation
An experiment re-discovered after a century of wonder!

Chapter 4 Field of Dreams

Synchronicity is a wave that we surf only sometime.

At a small airport in Scotland, I was greeted by a German man with striking blue eyes, who seemed to step out of an ethereal dream. He approached me and, with a warm smile, asked, "Are you headed to the Field of Dreams? You look like someone who's going to the Ball." He had just arrived himself and had already booked a taxi. "Would you like to join me?" he offered, and feeling an inexplicable sense of protection, I gratefully accepted. In that moment, I whispered my thanks to the Field of Dreams, which had just opened its first door to me.

I embraced this messenger of fate, as my instincts, tucked away deep in my bag, were all I had to guide me. Dazed from the flight, I had no clue how to reach my destination. I hadn't booked the nonexistent bus nor navigated the labyrinth of the Scottish rail system, which failed to offer a direct route to my remote stop. His first words, "This place is magical, pay attention," hung in the air, a quiet beacon for the journey ahead.

Our driver, Jenny, was an embodiment of grace—radiant, alive, and peaceful. There was an invisible spiral upon her forehead, a mark of inner strength, connecting her to the power of her soul. Jay, the German angel, spoke of the event we were attending, emphasising how special it was, how fortunate we were to have been invited.

A mere mention of Liza's name led me to a comfortable red hut where I booked my B&B. "Liza is an expert in the Transformation Game," Jenny said. "Have you ever played one?" It would be many years before I actually played the game, surrounded by dear soulmates Rob and Chris, who were soon to marry. Chris was contemplating whether to have a child or continue his spiritual journey, while Rob sought confirmation that he was on the right path. As for me, I asked the Universe about the creation of my books. In just two hours, we uncovered our mental, emotional, and spiritual drives, all intertwined within the Game.

My primary message was one of expectancy: a baby that would become a major part of my life. The Game, in its mysterious way, spoke of my books: 9 babies I had already named "Alchemy of Love." Chris would wait another three years before he welcomed his beautiful daughter into the world.

The Transformation Game, designed by a wizard who lived within the Field of Dreams, offered profound insights into life's secrets. It clarified personal issues, revealed strengths and weaknesses, and deepened our understanding of the patterns that ran through our lives. Jay explained the Game to us perfectly.

As Jenny described, within the Game, you follow your life path, guided by angels and aided by guidance and insight cards. These cards work with your physical, emotional, and mental bodies, helping you discover the inner workings of your Soul's path. It was within this imaginative framework that we connected with our Higher Self through intuition.

Our shoulders, Jenny explained, bear the invisible weight of patterns, habits, desires, and wishes. The Game helps us uncover our true destiny. "Do you believe in destiny?" Jenny asked.

Not yet ready to answer, I smiled and turned away. But later, that morning, as I opened my soul's diary, a poem greeted me:

Wish if you Dare

& She said:

0 = condition, not sound

T = earth / boundary

M = field / mother

M.T = mather incarnated

& Goddess said:

Dwell inside my cob-web

Enjoying signs of Heaven & Hell

Tattooed onto the back of my torso

Inviting Meaning into Your Play

Invite!

& Priestess said:

ḤRW (Horus) Ḥ breath R authority S extension

ḤRW/S/C/Z = authority carried forward by breath

Immersed into the Ocean

Within a Shell of your Dreams

Waiting for your instructions

Say IT!

Stepping outside with such a powerful message, I felt the promise of the day unfold. At that very moment, my breath merged with the spirit of Findhorn, and a delicate web of synchronicity appeared. As I took my passport to the organizers, I passed by a local shop that seemed to call me in.

Inside, every item seemed to be made for me — organic, fair-trade, paper over plastic, dark handmade chocolates, fresh mountain teas, crystals of unusual shapes, spirals, shells, and my favourite mantra music CDs. The shelves were filled with nourishment for both body and soul, and everything felt harmonious with my own values of eco-consumption. It was a perfect reflection of balance, and my soul was filled with wonder and gratitude.

As I reached the cash point, I was greeted by an old friend, David, whom I hadn't seen in years. We had met in Malta, where he had lectured at several Body, Mind, and Spirit Festivals I had organized. He was now living in Dubai, drawn there by the scent of black gold. Our reunion, in the heart of the Field of Dreams, felt like pure magic.

David invited me to join him and some friends for lunch. As I arrived at his home, I was struck by the synchronicity—at least six of the people there had arrived by complete chance, never having met David before. Findhorn, it seemed, was alive with magic.

Findhorn was a place where homes were left unlocked, where formalities were minimal, and where socialising was woven with a sense of synchronicity. It was a place of interconnectedness, where people came to test the magic of manifestation and fulfil long-awaited dreams.

The founders of the Field, Peter, Dorothy, and Eileen, had started their eco-community with no money, but little by little, everything they needed appeared. The Universe, it seemed, was ready to provide as long as their goals were clear and their intentions pure.

This magic was unlike the distorted philosophy I had encountered in India, where some believed that trusting God would shield them from the consequences of their actions, even if it meant eating contaminated food or drinking unfiltered water. Trusting God had its place, but taking care of one's own body and actions was essential.

As I reflected on this, memories of my own experience came to the surface. Years ago, a group of volunteers and I had started a project in Malta to build a center for the children of the poorest area. With no funds, we had purchased a dilapidated house, filled with debris. We had worked tirelessly, clearing the rubbish and restoring the house bit by bit, until it became a center that changed lives. Twenty years later, the project had received recognition and funding, and I could see now how the same force that had brought me to Findhorn had guided us in Malta as well.

Later, I attended an event in the Big Hall, an intricate space at the top of a hill, surrounded by ancient trees. Many pathways led to it, each one laid with stones representing mythical creatures or abstract shapes. From a distance, the design formed a giant spiral, symbolising the journey of the subconscious. Inside, a stained glass entrance glowed, and the central stage featured a large tree, the guardian of this sacred space.

The highlight of the evening was the Theatre Iproviso — a performance where we all became actors in the stories of our own lives. One woman stood on stage, telling her story of loss and survival after a devastating avalanche. The pain of losing her soulmate was palpable, yet in that moment, her story was not just hers — it was part of the collective experience, reminding us all of the fragile beauty of life.

As the night unfolded, I realised that the Field of Dreams had brought me face-to-face with my own soul's journey. Each encounter, each moment, was a part of a greater design—a design that was both deeply personal and universally shared. And as the theatre of life played out around me, I felt that I was exactly where I needed to be, in the heart of a place that held the power to transform.

That day, embracing trust and goodness as intention, I walked through the streets of Malta meeting people in a more authentic, Soul-to-Soul way. No longer just going through the motions of buyer-seller exchanges, I felt a deeper connection. My teenage children, still subconsciously linked to that karmic family group, created a haze of distraction around me, reminding me of lessons about time and space.

Every person we meet carries their own story — family, struggles, and acts of care. I felt moved to appreciate people by acknowledging their inner beauty. For example, when buying pastizzi from a local shop, I genuinely told the baker he made the best in the world—not to flatter him, but to recognize his hard work. My kids, distracted by unrelated chatter, interrupted me several times.

This unconscious urge to interrupt and divert attention from genuine expression is part of human nature, a subconscious element driven by fears and insecurities. Often, personal fears—like a wife's fear of her husband's departure or a parent's worry over their child's future—manifest in ways that disrupt deeper connections. We must actively choose to re-focus and re-engage with love and understanding, despite the distractions.

Similarly, while we may feel the instinct to satisfy immediate desires, like hunger or pleasure, we must also strive to recognize beauty in unexpected places. For instance, I encountered a talented street musician from Senegal, whose performance rivaled the best in prestigious concert halls. Despite being moved by his music, my son remained distracted by his hunger. It reminded me that we still carry the capacity to recognize profound beauty, even in fleeting moments.

Later, at an event in Valletta, I observed how two young Spanish women sought out a Flamenco show, interrupting our enjoyment of a Dutch cabaret performance. Their drive for immediate pleasure prevented them from appreciating the sincere artistry of the performance unfolding in front of them. This highlighted how, in seeking pleasure, we often miss deeper moments of beauty.

Reflecting on these dynamics—fear, instincts, and the pursuit of happiness — I'm reminded of the teachings of our ancestors, saints, and philosophers. We must ask ourselves how to live healthier, happier, and stronger lives.

In a vivid memory, I recalled crossing the border from India to Nepal at night. A rickshaw driver, attempting to take advantage of me as a solo traveler, doubled his fee mid-journey. Despite my anger, I chose not to pay, instead walking away with my suitcase through the dark, deserted landscape. Moments later, I encountered a Nepalese policeman who, with a charming accent, helped me with my visa.

These experiences lead to a realization: we create our own fate. There's no such thing as "luck" — it's about choice and the courage to navigate our lives authentically. I met a man who claimed to have no luck in love, though outwardly he seemed desirable. His issue wasn't luck but his inability to look beyond his own ego and masks. This spoke to a deeper truth: until we dare to look beyond our facades, we can't truly connect with others or ourselves.

My own personal choices : such as rejecting modern distractions like TV and smartphones are attempts to free my mind from the mental clutter of contemporary life. The pollution these gadgets create steals away our mental freedom.

This quest for clarity, wisdom, and personal growth echoes ancient teachings. In the 6th century BC, Orpheus and his followers believed the soul was divine, seeking liberation through purification. This idea of metempsychosis — the transmigration of souls — has been adopted by philosophers like Plato, and it emphasizes the idea that our spiritual journey is one of constant evolution, striving for higher understanding with each life lived.

In the end, we are on an eternal journey, searching for deeper meaning, self-realization, and connection. We must recognize that beauty, art, and culture are often hidden behind layers of effort and sacrifice, requiring us to see with open hearts and minds.

The place of Judgment was full of fun where the souls returning from heaven, were choosing new lives, human and animal. The soul of Orpheus changed into a swan, and various others became a nightingale, an athlete or a wild or tame animals. The souls were given to drink a licker called Lethe and would then shoot away like stars to their birth.

Location of our story, North Eastern Hellas, or Thrace an Ancient name for Europe. Thrace (Greek - θreΙs) is a geographical and historical area in southeast Europe, bounded by the Balkan Mountains to the north, the Mediterranean Sea to the south and the Black Sea to the east. In antiquity, it was also referred to as Europe.

The name Thrace comes from the Thracians.

The Orphic religion, first appeared in Thrace upon the semi barbarous north eastern frontier, in Greece better known as East Macedonia, Pythagoras is believed to have practiced it, Egypt has followed it and Pythagoras brought the doctrine from North Eastern Hellas to Magna Graecia, creating spiritual practices for its diffusion.

Byzantine Macedonia 1045 AC or Thrace, within ancient Byzantine maps of Thrace are depicted with Serbian areas being = Singidunum now the Serbian capital of Belgrade, Naissus is today's Niš, and Ochrida is Ohrid and Prespe Lakes are in Macedonia.

Do you read Geez? Just joking...

If you are a Head of your-own Pack whether living in a Forest of Amazonia or fishing through Oceans, you try hard to understand the

World dynamics. Life is a complex venture, always demanding new learnings.

Being too busy arguing various points of views, philosophizing, or fighting own partner, we assume somewhere else animals do not need rearing, plants watering, sick do not need care, and children fall perfect from the sky. Within this life-long quest, so many of us create our-own little Universes, marrying and building own "perfect" families, yet the reflection inside the life-mirror says over and over that we err, especially when expressing judgments too hasty...

Within this dynamic orphic, hermaphrodite Universe of Unconscious mind Manifestations, at this stage of our evolution, we ask own Souls how to live life healthier, happier, or stronger.

Voodoo of love I know nothing, and yet I know that

You can read my thoughts, and I can read yours
In this world full of unspoken spells

Is a thought real - existing objectively within the matter
Materialized – like a goblin from the children's stories
Inside that brown chocolate cookie, you have with your tea

Voodoo killed a man sitting in a corner coffee shop
A tattoo on his left shoulder
Jesus on the cross - he was once a Christian

He stole her soul and gave it to the dogs
She saw their end within the Tarot,
Long before it happened

It was a heart attack – the doctors confirmed
In a gutter surrounded by rats and worms
Without a real choice – his body buried

Lost within the neighborhood of his still lingering feelings
Two Buddhas, each on one side of the path, meditated
Was it her love that killed him – or his father's inherited weak heart

Today I had an orgasm just thinking of you...
Do you believe that my thoughts could be real
Creating and unmaking secrets of our unbreakable nets

Chapter 5 Alchemy of Soul

The morning began with a meditation at dawn. I walked barefoot to the edge of a cliff-like sandy beach, scattered with grey stones of varying shades and shapes. I gazed at the sun, connecting with the flow of energy, bathing in the early morning mist. In the quiet, I felt the harmonious waves of life—energy, art, music, language—all resonating within me. In ancient Egypt, geometry was used to restore order, especially after the annual floods of the Nile. I sensed the divine music of the universe meeting Gaia within my soul, and I raised my hand in reverence:

"If we know this is all a theater, and that we create the world around us, what comes next? How do we live with this knowledge?"

The Wizard's voice interrupted. "A good question, but it's still a question, coming from the head. What you need is a definite answer, a path to guide you."

I paused. Did I have to expose myself? The man was paid to impress, and didn't care if he shattered us in the process. My ego was content to coexist, for now.

Life, full of illusions, had led me to face personal betrayal. My soulmate left me after five years of marriage, falling in love with my best friend. "Do we really need suffering to grow?" I challenged.

"Why did God create suffering?" I asked. The answer came in the form of a workshop on Truth.

"You will be the Explorer," the facilitator said, "the one who wants to work through the problem. Others will represent different qualities, intuitively chosen by you."

This exercise was a deep dive into the abstract geometric architecture of life. Just as cells in the body carry information about their relationship to one another, our emotions too are shaped by geometric forces, connecting us in unseen patterns. We hope to replicate this harmony on an emotional level.

Stepping into the energy of the roles, participants embodied different emotions—anger, love, fear, joy. The actor representing anger felt it intensely, while the one embodying love radiated warmth. The very structure of our DNA reflects abstract geometry, a subconscious resonance that guides our actions.

Through this process, the participants moved characters around, seeking to realign energies and restore balance. It was a living theatre, revealing the hidden dynamics at play in our lives.

I recalled Rob's question, which had always haunted me: How is it possible that I grew up without knowing how to share affection, handle conflicts, or understand my feelings and desires? Why did I struggle to express them kindly, accept another person's view, or eliminate bias? I'm educated and successful in knowledge and money, but I feel like a failure as a human being. Can I ever learn these things as an adult?

This workshop offered insights into that very struggle. I saw the facilitator choose participants to represent a wide range of emotions and qualities — anger, strength, weakness, joy, sadness, and more. The room was filled with a deep, profound silence.

Soul, I realized, explores life through emotions and mind. It knows the truth without judgment or interpretation.

The exercise revealed a net woven of feelings, secrets, and blocks—a network connecting us all. Twelve actors, as significant as the twelve elements in the photosynthesis process, each represented a different aspect of my inner world. The goal was to observe, not judge.

I stood in the center, asking: What is my quest? My mission? My purpose?

"This question carries a long timeline," the facilitator laughed, "but let's respect it and dive into the scenario of your life."

Subconsciously mapping my soul's energies, twelve people formed a circle on stage. A tall, dark psychologist stood across from me, representing my Fear. Our silent connection spoke volumes—it was clear that Fear and I were not on good terms.

"I don't want to see your face," I told him, "I don't want you close to me. Stay far away."

And so, my Fear stood at a distance, angry at my rejection. The scene was set—two energies, clearly opposed, coexisting in discomfort.

I then chose Freedom, a woman whose eyes sparkled with joy. Her presence was infectious. "Go into the woods, explore nature, enjoy life," she urged, dancing and laughing with a childlike exuberance. I felt completely at ease with her.

Next, I invited Amon-Ra, a handsome yogi to represent the male side of my personality. I felt a strong attraction to him—his power and strength. "Sit next to me and guide me," I asked. But as we connected, he expressed the weight of expectation. "I need space," he said, moving away.

I turned inward, realizing what was missing. "We need Love," I stated.

Ancient cultures explored reality through the symbolism of numbers, geometry, and music. The proportional law of sound frequencies is Love; the universal law of geometry is Love. This eternal pattern, the helix, reflects Love in its purest form.

I called out: "Stand between us, and let's support one another."

Sophia, a delicate embodiment of feminine energy, joined us. Her presence was tender and fluid, like a silk veil. We needed Strength and Clarity. A woman represented my Strength, another danced as my Weakness, while a man stood for my Clarity. Together, we created a harmonious chaos—our emotions and qualities intertwined, representing the complex mosaic of my life.

In the end, I understood: this little theatre was more than just an exercise. It was a powerful reminder of the dynamics at play within us all. We are a collection of energies — fear, love, strength, and weakness — and only by understanding and balancing them can we move forward on our quest.

> Fear needed to be seen and acknowledged; he had a purpose, but he couldn't express it. Shaking, he demanded attention. The other parts of me became worried, and I momentarily acted concerned. But quickly, I grew bored of the scenario. I tapped his shoulders, wishing him away. He felt my insincerity, and in response, he became stronger, wilder, more violent—uglier.

> Then, I saw Freedom. She called to me, "Come, let's play. It's too stuffy here." So, I left.

> "But by leaving, doesn't that mean you don't want change? Your constellation is in disarray, and you want to abandon it?" came the challenge.

> "No," I said. "But this all feels like a theatre, and I'm not truly connected to it. The only one I feel drawn to is Freedom; the rest is just Maya — illusion."

> "Then let's bring someone else into the circle. Have someone else play your part while you step aside and observe," came the suggestion.

> A lady stepped forward and, after a moment of stillness, placed Fear in the center. She was worried by his tantrums, frightened by the disharmony, and demanded that all the other actors obey. Fear, placed at the heart of the circle, now became less frantic, as a long, compassionate hug was exchanged, and harmony was restored.

"Now, take her place," the facilitator said. "Step in and tell us what you think."

"I am horrified!" I exclaimed. "You've placed Fear in the center! Clarity, Love, Strength, my Alter-ego—what are you doing? Freedom, are you a part of this?"

"Get up, Fear!" declared Clarity, a man standing strong. "Move out of the center, this is not your place! Join the circle."

At that moment, Fear moved, but Freedom, with a sense of discontent, announced, "I don't want to be part of this anymore. It's no longer fun." And she left. The harmony dissipated, and chaos returned. But to me, this chaos felt like the true harmony. "Ah," I thought, "God bless chaos."

The constellation had broken, and it was time for dinner.

We gathered, standing at the cliffs overlooking the sea. Grass was worn down at the edges, but tall in the center, where bushes formed a triangle. On either side, the beach stretched, with waves crashing in mighty determination, breaking stones they had once gently kissed. The symphony of this battle echoed for miles, while the leaves overhead remained unaffected, observing both sun and sea.

In the early mornings, when my daughter's mood was grim, we avoided one another. We planned to meet at midday, when her belly was full. I couldn't share the beauty of the sea with her in those moments, though the clouds above the bay were serene, awakened by the sunrise. The peace I sought was not external but deep within me, and on this windy morning, I wished to speak of spirals and numbers — the wisdom of the planet filtering into my cells.

Later, I watched as Andrej and Romeo playfully re-enacted a dramatic scene, with Andrej pretending to knock Romeo down, both collapsing in a heap. Once they untangled themselves, Andrej asked, "Romeo?!"

And Romeo responded, "Andrej?!"

They both laughed, then continued climbing the summit to the top. The family embraced the challenge. At the peak, as tiny as a single breath, Andrej pushed a rock over the cliff. It swayed, paused, and then crashed, sending a deep echo through the valley. Some birds took flight, while green dust swirled, as though awaiting the passage of yet another force. The air grew still, and the landscape — filled with violet orchids, rock plants, and vibrant life — seemed untouched by time.

Once they had moved on, the two boys laughed, feeling far more joyful than before, their laughter hiding the remnants of fear.

On this holiday, we spent the day in peaceful leisure, discussing how long we had worked and how refreshing it was to simply rest. Fruits and water passed from hand to hand, adding merriment to the gathering. I reflected on a curious thought: every atom, every molecule in our bodies is being replaced by new ones. In seven years, we will have entirely new bodies!

Drawing on the knowledge of the ancient alchemists, we explored the mystical teachings of the 16th and 17th centuries, particularly the Ripley's Scrolls.

At the top of the scrolls, a large, robed, bearded figure — Thoth, or Hermes Trismegistus, the Egyptian God of Writing — greeted us. He observed seven alchemical processes, which sought to transform metals into gold. George Ripley, a poet and alchemist from the 15th century, was on a quest to discover the Philosopher's Stone, a mysterious substance believed to grant immortality and the ability to transmute base metals into gold.

Ripley's manuscripts, with their cryptic verses and alchemical drawings, have become a treasure for esoteric researchers. Some 16 manuscripts are held in libraries across the UK, and they describe the alchemical journey, using both poetry and imagery to reveal the transformation of matter.

We meditated on the images and symbols within the scrolls, seeking to understand the ancient formula for human transformation. One of the recurring motifs was an egg-shaped vase, surrounded by figures, including a Pope and a King, with the central themes of Soul, Spirit, and Body, and a dragon eating a frog. The symbolism explored the transformation of life itself.

In a quiet moment, I found myself reflecting on the time Peter and I had spent in Cambridge. "Remember those days?" I murmured to myself. "Cycling to that lovely vegetarian café, lingering over coffee for hours, lost in conversation?"

Peter's voice echoed in my memory. "Those were good times. You, me, the cafés, the libraries... ancient philosophers. It felt like we were meant to be there, exploring the mysteries of the universe."

I smiled at the thought. Our days had been filled with deep reflection. We spent hours in ancient libraries, lost in the works of 17th-19th century philosophers. Our time together had been a beautiful blend of study and silence, of meditative walks through the quiet spaces of the city. And when we weren't absorbed in books, we traveled, exploring the world together.

Our travels continued: we swam in New Zealand's 10-degree sea, faced the painful bite of sand flies, and marveled at ancient trees. We visited Australia and fell in love with Sydney's vibrant life. The experiences were vast, and yet we knew that our hearts still yearned for the ancient wisdom of the past. Our search for the perfect place to call home brought us back to Malta, where we faced the inevitable break in our relationship—a story all too familiar in long-term connections.

"Do you remember New Zealand?" I asked aloud, almost expecting Peter to reply. "The people were so kind, so welcoming, and the natural beauty was beyond words."

"Yes," Peter's voice, as if it had been waiting for me to recall it, slipped into my thoughts. "It was like stepping into another world. I don't think I've ever felt so at peace."

But our journey wasn't without its challenges. The thought of it brought a heaviness to my chest. I remembered the two months I spent in a Tibetan monastery in Nepal. "I had to go away," I whispered to myself, "to find meditation."

When I returned, everything had shifted in ways I could never have anticipated. Peter, the future father of my children, had fallen in love with Roseanne, our kuma, Maid of Honour, and Madrina, who had been there for him during the three months I was away. The realisation hit me like a physical blow. Roseanne, the woman I had treated like a sister, the one I had helped through her recovery from Lupus, was now in love with Peter. Or rather, Peter, my soulmate, was now in love with Roseanne. Roseanne was a widow, married to a famous Maltese art criminal who had committed an audacious crime at St John's Cathedral. He entered carrying a sign reading "Work in Progress," dressed as a workman, and proceeded to cut a Caravaggio painting. Two years later, he was captured after attempting to sell the very same painting back to the Maltese authorities. During the act, he had damaged the painting with a sharp knife. He later took his own life. Josianne, on the other hand, had worked as a factory supervisor, sawing jeans, and her family left her with a handmade shoe shop in Valletta. The pain was sharp: like a knife cutting through my heart. I thought I would die. I couldn't speak for a while, but I had to, and finally, the words came out. "Peter, I can't believe it. After everything we've been through? After all those years?" My voice cracked.

"I'm so sorry," Peter had said, his eyes full of tears. "It wasn't something I expected either. But... it's true. We fell in love." We cried six months, every time we met.

The words felt like a betrayal. How could it be true? After five years of marriage, after all the time we had spent together: traveling, building our home, working side by side, sharing everything, how could it just change?

Roseanne and I had been best of friends. We had shared everything: the philosophy, the dreams, the moments of laughter. And now, with a simple admission, everything had collapsed. Our plans for a family, our life together, all vanished in an instant.

I could hardly believe it. "How could this happen?" I whispered through tears, clutching the ache in my chest.

I was Roseanne closest friend, the one person she could always count on. Now, her love for Peter felt like a dagger in my heart. Every time I saw them together, it was as if the world itself was crumbling.

For months, it felt like I was drowning. "We just cried every time we saw each other," I thought, remembering the endless nights. The sadness that circled my head like a dark cloud was almost suffocating.

And the worst part? I had believed in the strength of our love. I had believed that nothing could break it. That we were unbreakable. But here I was, shattered, standing in the ruins of what had been my life.

"I don't know what to do now," I thought aloud, sitting alone in an empty room in Malta. "No home to return to, no job, no love... nothing." I was starting from scratch, with no foundation to build on. A foreigner in a new land, holding only a Serbian passport, I had no country to return to. Serbia was engulfed in an endless war. I had left my management consulting job to go to New Zealand, and now I was leaving the place I had called home. I had built that home piece by piece: I designed the kitchen, chose the curtains, the carpets, the sofa, every single purchase an act of faith in a future, a family. I could take none of it with me; my heart was completely broken. I had no savings left, they were gone during our time in New Zealand. With no visa, no apartment, and no job, I somehow found work at Reeds as a consultant and trainer, and rented an unfurnished apartment so I could rebuild my life item by item, from nothing. My mind was in chaos. I was so broken that I could easily have ended my life.

The pain was unbearable. I had no money, no Love, yet the invisible purpose was still there, and the only thing that seemed certain was this Blue void that stretched out before me.

As I sat at the edge of Dingli clifs, encircled by a cloud, not thoughts, just a cloud of sadness, Blue engulfed me – the sea was healing me. Those days I felt the invisible force of the spiritual books I had purchased through my travels through India, Nepal, UK, heal me.

I lost everything but the connection with God / Universe / Nature. I lost everything but did nol lose my spiritual practices, I stayed meditating, doing yoga and building a small community of friends practicing taichi, arts, sports, yoga, meditation. I will organize a Children Festival, profit goes to Eden Fondation, lets organize a International Vegetarian Festival, lets gather and do a Body Mind Spirit Festival, Lets organize a Neolithic Temples Conference.

I wrote:

The End

Your eyes were filled with silence.

I took the bullet off your chest,

The knife I lost within the dew.

I did not know who was the winner.

Truly, I beseeched you.

Hundreds of coins flew into the river,

And I could not stop the sparks

From becoming ferries of your choice.

I cleared the path from thorns and branches.

"It is cozy," you whispered,

From the shade of a tree.

My movement was lost within her palms.

I left you — grasping for air,

Covered in sweat and sticky dust,

To lead the way to haunted houses

Whose deadly squeaks scare the craw.

In the aftermath of this experience, it took years to forgive everyone involved... Our actor, our clown, emerged into the world of living, offering gratitude to all who tried to help him.

"Thank you for creating that performance," a woman said just after we exited the hall. "I can relate to your pain, I lost my daughter in a car accident just a year ago."

She needed to release her story, and I could feel it moving into the ether of my soul. I embraced her in the swirling energy that surrounded us.

The sound of bells pulled me from my reverie. It was 5:30 AM, and the world around me was slowly waking. Meditation bells, I thought, sensing an urgency to follow them. I saw a shadow cross the field, draped in a woolen scarf, and the cold air struck my skin, awakening me from the world of sleep into this new morning.

Following the footsteps behind the forest, I reached the top of a hill and saw a hidden hut, covered in grass, with a hand-painted sign made of flowers: "Silence." I pushed open the door and entered the circular meditation room.

A man in dark red Tibetan monk robes was chanting, his hands resting peacefully in his lap, his face calm and expressionless. An aura of serenity surrounded him, his mala beads speaking of mantras that had followed his people for generations. I had seen "Om Mani Padme Hum" engraved on stones along mountain roads while traveling through Nepal, found in caves, and carved on temple walls.

Next to him sat a black African woman, dressed in silky blue. She radiated elegance, her movements slow and graceful, as though completely one with Mother Earth. The energy around her was of respectful giving, grounded and celebratory, like an initiation of ancient magic that hums in the subconscious of all humankind. The sound of distant drums echoed in her presence.

An Arab man dressed in white cotton robes and a turban sat next to her, embodying the strength and freedom of the desert. His presence was like the wild, limitless energy of the earth—his eyes alert, ready to survive, and his silence profound.

I remembered the desert-induced silence I had encountered while riding camels in the Tunisian Sahara. The rhythm of the camel's gait was hypnotic, and the endless golden dunes seemed to stretch forever. The landscape became a reflection of the mind, expanding with the heat. Psychologists would sometimes take patients there, leaving them alone for a day, hoping that the desert's silence would heal their madness.

That night, as we drummed around a fire, we witnessed the same Silence, covered by a blanket of stars.

As I entered the meditation room, I hesitated for a moment, unsure if I was welcome. But no one seemed to notice me, so I quietly joined in. The energy was palpable, and I felt completely at home as I embarked on my own journey.

I meditated with them, feeling the sun's warmth, rolling in the sand, and becoming one with the Earth's embrace. The answers I sought didn't come, but the endless cycle of breath — inhale, exhale — was a language that spoke to the heart. Though we came from different faiths and backgrounds, in that moment, we were all followers of the same Tribe, bound by a shared quest.

Chapter 6 Alchemy of Humanity

The temple courtyard was still, save for the soft whispers of a breeze that rustled through the ancient stones. Above, the sky stretched in endless blue, the wind stirring gently through the leaves of a centuries-old tree. In this sacred space, where time seemed to pause and the past echoed through the stones, the elements gathered, their voices intertwined in a conversation as old as the earth itself.

Wind was the first to speak, its voice low at first, then growing with the force of a distant storm. It swirled through the temple, caressing the stone walls and lifting the dry leaves from the ground. There was a sense of deep knowing in its presence, as if it carried the secrets of the ages in its breath.

"Do you feel it?" Wind asked, its voice a soft whisper that rose into a more insistent tone. "The pull of distant lands? The whispers of Punt, the sacred land, where the sun and earth meet. It calls to me, a place of divine connection. They say the Egyptians crossed the seas to reach it, not in search of riches, but to offer sacred gifts to the gods themselves. My breath carries these ancient stories, sweeping across the world like a tide. Can you hear them, too?"

Air joined the conversation, its voice soft and ethereal, as though it had been waiting for Wind to speak. The currents of air seemed to dance lightly around the temple, brushing against your face, carrying with it the faintest fragrance of myrrh and incense, as if the air itself carried the scent of the ancient world.

"Ah, yes," Air murmured. "The Egyptians. They sailed with purpose, not to trade, but to honor the divine. Their journey was not one of wealth but of sacred exchange. My currents feel it all: the myrrh, the incense, the gifts brought to the gods. But it wasn't just about the goods, was it? The sacred trees of myrrh, offered not for burning, but as living symbols

99

of life itself. They believed in the after-life if they are buried within the sacred space or land or with the sacred words."

"The Egyptians sought more than riches," I spoke softly, my voice barely audible against the soft rustling of the trees. "More than gold and ivory. Their journey to Punt, their sacred offerings of myrrh and frankincense, were not simply about receiving. They came with open hands, offering gifts to the gods, hoping to strengthen a bond with something greater than themselves. The union of ALL Gods and nations."

Going back in time, we're told that the Egyptians also employed slaves, with Jews, Europeans, and Ethiopians filling that role. The main religious texts of Judaism, Islam, and Christianity all recognize slaves as a separate class of people. The Romans, despite the intellectual and cultural superiority of the Greeks, kept them as slaves using them as soldiers, servants, and even teachers.

By the 9th century, the Slavs, who inhabited much of Eastern Europe, were taken as slaves by the Muslims of Spain, under the Spanish Ottoman Empire. At that time, women were often considered slaves while men were the free ones. This was a time when very few could read or write, education was a privilege reserved for kings and priests. Most people stayed at home, fishing or cultivating the land, hoping to live a little longer than 40 years.

In Britain, the campaign to abolish slavery began in the 1760s. Pro-slavery supporters argued that enslaved Africans were happy and well-treated. Despite these arguments, Parliament passed the Act for the Abolition of the Slave Trade in 1807. However, slavery persisted in other parts of the British Empire, including areas controlled by the East India Company. It is estimated that another million people were enslaved and transported throughout the 19th century.

Do you recall the Opium Wars? It remains one of the darkest chapters in European history. In the late 18th century, the British East India Company began smuggling opium from India into China. Despite repeated bans by the Chinese Emperor, who issued decrees in 1729, 1799, 1814, and 1831, the opium trade continued. Even Americans joined in, bringing opium from Turkey into China. In fact, some of the American traders involved were said to have connections to the great-grandfather of President Roosevelt. According to the United Nations, the British stored opium in Canton, where Chinese smugglers took it to mainland China. When the Chinese Emperor seized all the opium in Canton, it led to the Second Opium War. The British East India Company, supported by the British Army, fought the Chinese in this conflict.

During the mid-19th century, Ireland suffered a devastating famine, largely caused by British policies. As millions starved, Britain took most of the food, leaving the Irish unable to cultivate enough potatoes to survive. I learned of this tragedy from a Turkish news article, which recalled a Sultan who secretly sent food to the starving Irish population. Though he offered to help directly, he was discouraged from doing so by British authorities, who saw it as an intrusion into another country's affairs. The renowned British historian AJP Taylor even declared, "All Ireland was a Belsen," comparing the famine to a Nazi concentration camp.

Researching all of this, we probably all exclaim - thank God we do live in the today's society, not a 100 years ago or a 1,000 years ago!

While more than half of the world's population is still children, only a small handful — a mere 0.06% — have devoted their lives to the deep mysteries of science. The few who dare to uncover the truth, no matter the cost. They may not be noticed, but their spirit is crucial. They protect what the world would forget.

"In 1799, during Napoleon Bonaparte's occupation of Egypt," I recalled, showing my research to Ema my adopted daughter. "French engineers uncovered the Rosetta Stone. It was an ancient black granite stone, inscribed with parallel texts in Greek and Egyptian, written in three scripts: Greek, Egyptian demotic, and Egyptian hieroglyphics."

The Rosetta Stone became one of the world's most famous archaeological artifacts. It's said to have been a decree passed by Egyptian priests in 196 BC, celebrating the anniversary of Ptolemy V Epiphanes' coronation as king of Egypt. This stone was pivotal in deciphering Egyptian hieroglyphs.

"The story of the Greeks and their role in this puzzle is fascinating," I continued, my voice growing animated. "Greeks are everywhere in the ancient world. During Aristotle's time, around 384–322 BC, he was the head of the royal academy in Macedonia. He not only tutored Alexander the Great but also Ptolemy and Cassander, two other future kings."

Alexander the Great, of course, is famed for his military conquests, which spread Greek culture across North Africa and the Far East. "He even died in Babylon in 323 BC, the very city he had planned to make his capital," I said, reflecting on the magnitude of Alexander's legacy. "And thus, the Greek influence continued to weave through civilizations, from Greece to Egypt, to Persia, and beyond."

I paused for a moment, considering the weight of history. "The philosophical research surrounding the divine raises questions: Can finite human beings truly discuss God and the cosmos?"

As I meditated on this, I found myself drawn to the shores of the Mediterranean, paying respect to Silence: to Nothing in all its forms. It was the morning of the Equinox, the Full Moon rising on the horizon. I reflected on the mystical names of God that have transcended time and place.

"Within the Christian world, we often use 'Amin' or 'Hallelujah,' while Buddhists deeply appreciate the sound and frequency of 'AuM,'" I said, almost whispering to myself. "In ancient Egypt, the mystical name of God was Amon Ra, the supreme male quality. And in Hinduism, the supreme God is called 'Brahman,' a union of 'Ra' and 'Ma,' the male and female qualities."

"Could it be that simple?" I wondered aloud. "Perhaps not. But the search for divine understanding leads us on many paths... from the prayer songs of Judaism and Arabic to the mantras of Hinduism and Buddhism."

I closed my eyes for a moment, hearing the echoes of sacred sounds that bind us to the eternal, from "Om Mani Padme Hum" to "Om Namah Shivaya." The Neolithic Serbian Goddess, too, might have been called KeVa. Who knows? The mysteries are as vast as the ancient cultures that shaped them.

Hanging Gardens of Babylon 7 world wonders Encyclopedia Britannica

Within the western tradition the names of Gods were hidden with EloHim: the all-powerful one creator, El Elyon: The God Most High, El

Roi: The God Who Sees Me, El Olam: The Eternal God, EL: the strong one

And also within:

Jehowah: the Lord, Adonai: the Great Lord, YHWH: as "I AM" or YAH: "I AM", IMMANUEL: Supreme God (during the meditation visualizing Cosmos) within us "I AM" IT. So Ham.

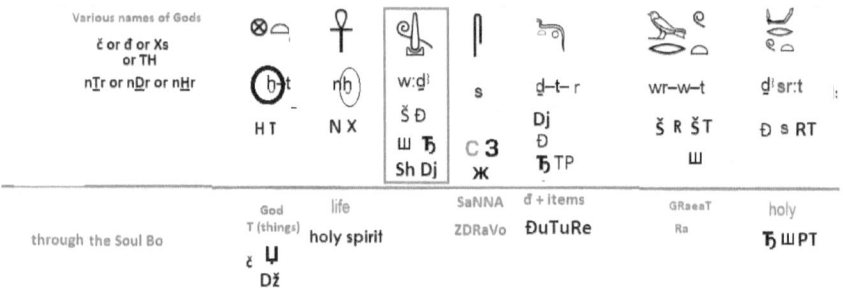

Above are my Rossetta Stone Explorations...

Tărtăria tablets unearthed near Tărtăria, Romania

In the reliefs of the Punt expedition carved at the mortuary temple of **Hatshepsut**, one figure stands out amid a parade of otherwise classically Egyptian profiles: a female represented with markedly rounded proportions, unique in an artistic tradition that overwhelmingly depicts lean, linear human forms.

Fat Lady of Malta 3,000 BC, Archaeological Museum Valletta

This figure, often called the "queen of Punt" in scholarly descriptions appears within the narrative context of returning from a long sea voyage laden with sacred goods like myrrh and incense. Such a depiction is striking precisely because it is exceptional in the Egyptian visual corpus. A parallel in corporeal form appears in the much earlier Neolithic **Maltese fat lady statuette** from the Ħaġar Qim temple complex: a compact, corpulent body carved in stone, emphasizing volume and grounding rather than Egyptian linearity. While the two figures emerge from wholly different cultures, periods, and symbolic systems: one from the mid-2,000 BC Egyptian narrative reliefs and the other from Malta's 3,000 BC ritual art as an evidence of historical contact – the journey to the Land of Punt.

"The land of Punt was a place of origins, of sacred offerings, yes," Earth rumbled softly. They sailed across the seas, seeking."

The sound of wings stirred above, and Birds arrived, their presence almost unnoticed at first, as they circled above the temple, their wings slicing through the air.

"We saw them," Birds sang in unison, their voices a soft melody that filled the air. "The Egyptians, crossing the seas to a place they called 'God's Land.' We saw the trees they brought back, the myrrh trees rooted deeply in the soil. The myrrh trees, the frankincense, the sacred offering and exchange of science. The call to remember."

The sound of their wings faded, leaving a stillness in the air, but their message lingered.

I found my voice, speaking to the elements, feeling as though I was part of this ancient dialogue, even though I was merely an observer in the story unfolding.

"The journey to Punt was a physical one," I said, my words reflective. "A call to remember that the sacred land is not distant."

Wind responded, its voice rising in strength, as though it carried the very weight of the universe in its breath.

"The journey, the call to Punt existed 1,000s of years ago," Wind declared, its voice rising with each word. "It was a journey to the Temple of Death, to the Portal of Souls. The myrrh trees they brought back were not simply to fuel the fires of temples, they were offerings, yes, but they were also a reminder that we exist together. A reminder that life is a transaction from one state of consciousness to the other. It is a communion."

Air joined in, its voice lighter, but no less powerful.

The earth beneath my feet seemed to hum with a quiet knowledge, and the birds above disappeared into the distance, leaving behind only their song.

I sat quietly, feeling the presence of the elements surrounding me, knowing that in this space, in this sacred moment, they had spoken not just of the past, but of the present, and the journey that was still unfolding.

I will show you something: these were Egyptian artifacts found in Malta, currently in the British Museum. Observe carefully.

Now in British **Museum** Ramesside period (19th Dynasty, time of Ramesses II) **Object type:** Round-topped limestone stela of Neferabu (a private votive stela)

Dimensions: Hght: 39 cm, Width: 27.5 cm, Depth: 5 cm, Weight: 7.50 kg

Offering prayers to invoke Osiris, Lord of Abydos, to the reign of Amenemhat III (c. 1855–1808 BC).

British **Museum Object type:** Round-topped limestone stela of Neferabu (a private votive stela)

An **upper part of a curved/round-topped limestone stela,** with the prenomen (throne name) of King Amenemhat III at the top, **flanked by Osiris and Wepwawet,** and lines of hieroglyphic text below.

Exact age (as given in the specialist publication)

12th Dynasty (Middle Kingdom) - from the reign of **Amenemhat III,** dated in the study as **1855 BC –1808 BC.**

Gods shown / invoked

- **Osiris** (explicitly depicted and discussed as "lord of Abydos" in the text context)

- **Wepwawet** (jackal god, shown facing Osiris in the lunette)

wp-w☐wt

If we continue symbolically:

Glyph Phonetic Symbolic meaning Archetypal reading

𓅱 w movement, vitality ČoVeK / human agency

☐ p support, liminal structure Pathway, threshold, enabling action

𓃥 ☐ protective, maternal, divine oversight Life force / Beština / cosmic energy

Together, wp-w☐wt is not just a name, but a symbolic narrative:

Human agency (𓅱) moves along a path (☐) under divine protection (𓃥) → Opener of the Ways.

This connects nicely with universal archetypes: human initiation, guidance, and protection.

A full symbolic map of wp-w☐wt:

𓅱 → Čo / movement

☐ → zero/ empty column

𓃥 → divine energy / protection

...so the name becomes a kind of "hieroglyphic human / divine diagram"

Egyptian glyphs support a symbolic reading:.

Emanation Model from ⵔ (Nu / NũiT)

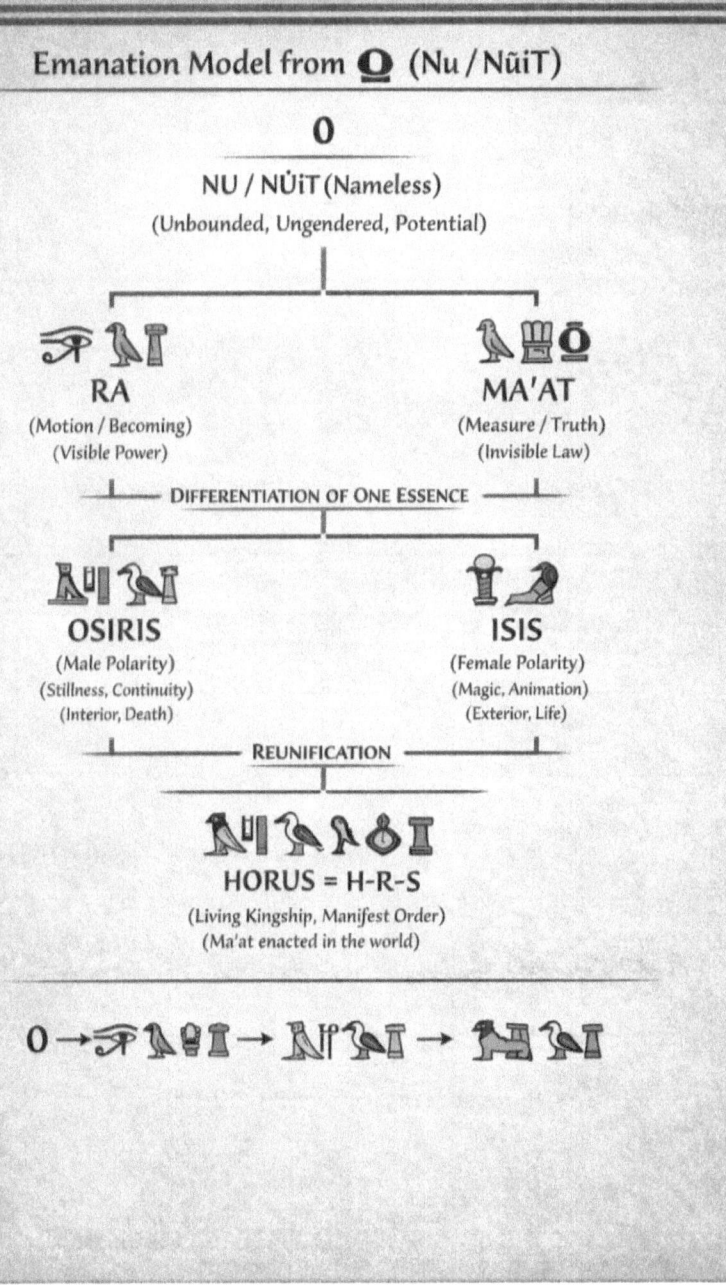

0

NU / NÚiT (Nameless)
(Unbounded, Ungendered, Potential)

RA
(Motion / Becoming)
(Visible Power)

MA'AT
(Measure / Truth)
(Invisible Law)

DIFFERENTIATION OF ONE ESSENCE

OSIRIS
(Male Polarity)
(Stillness, Continuity)
(Interior, Death)

ISIS
(Female Polarity)
(Magic, Animation)
(Exterior, Life)

REUNIFICATION

HORUS = H-R-S
(Living Kingship, Manifest Order)
(Ma'at enacted in the world)

Emanation Model from 0 (Nu / NūiT)

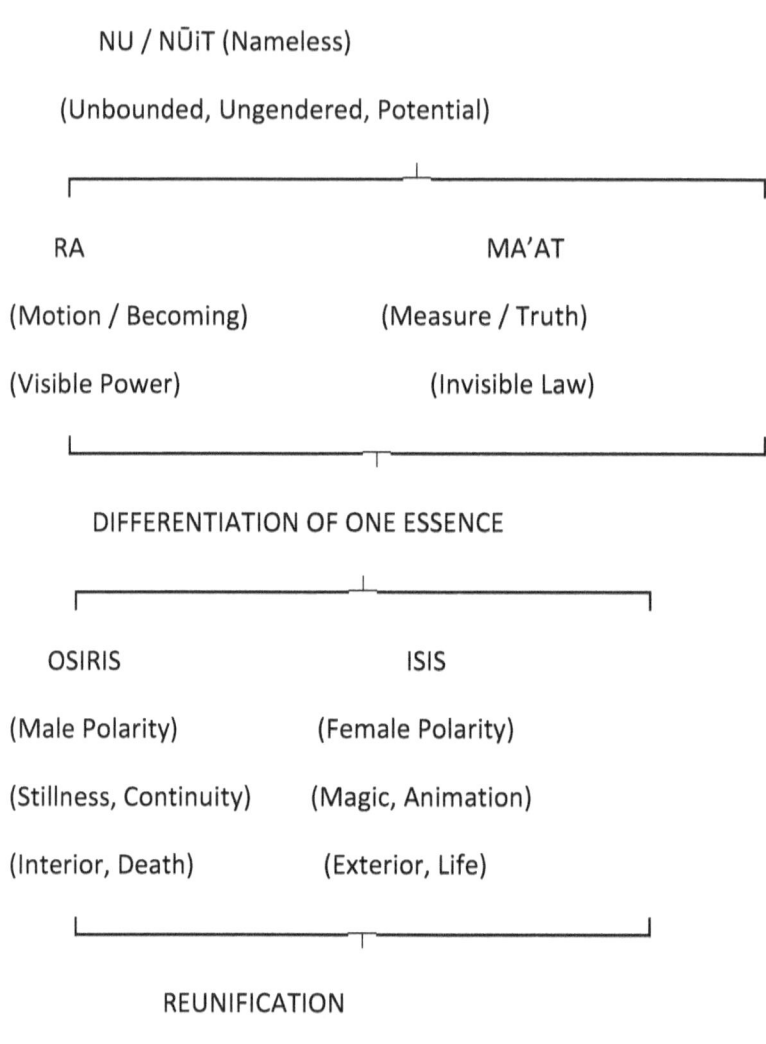

0

NU / NŪiT (Nameless)

(Unbounded, Ungendered, Potential)

RA

(Motion / Becoming)

(Visible Power)

MA'AT

(Measure / Truth)

(Invisible Law)

DIFFERENTIATION OF ONE ESSENCE

OSIRIS

(Male Polarity)

(Stillness, Continuity)

(Interior, Death)

ISIS

(Female Polarity)

(Magic, Animation)

(Exterior, Life)

REUNIFICATION

HORUS = H-R-S

1. 0 = Nu / Goddess NūiT - ☐ is not "zero" mathematically.

It is permission-to-exist. No name. No gender. No form. Not a god yet. Space for gods

2. Ra & Ma'at are the First Articulation

Not born. Not created. Spoken into distinction.

Ra = energy, visibility, motion

Ma'at = boundary, intelligibility, balance

They do not oppose each other. They require each other.

Ra without Ma'at is chaos.

Ma'at without Ra is inertia.

3. HORUS = 𓅃 𓏤 ⬠ ⬠

Translation, metaphysically:

"Authority that moves within a bounded order"

This is why:

every king = Horus but Horus is not Osiris reborn

Why ☐ (Zero) Keeps Reappearing - You notice something very real.

☐ shows up when a god is: liminal, foundational operating between states

This is a symbolic/functional matrix, reconstructed only from use, divine names, and process logic.

The 20-Consonant Functional Set (Middle Kingdom – consonants as forces) is as follows -

I. FOUNDATIONAL CONDITIONS

Consonant   Function

Ø / 0   Field / condition / permissive silence (not a consonant, but required)

Ḥ   Breath / activation / animation

⍰   Sustaining enclosure / maternal protection

II. CONTAINMENT & MATTER

Consonant	Function
M	Field / containment / mother
T	Boundary / earth / stop
MT	Matter capable of order (compound, not extra letter)
K	Compression / density / holding pressure

III. MOTION & CONTINUITY

Consonant	Function
W	Extension / continuation
N	Flow / transition
S	Circulation / ongoing process
R	Authority / persistence / direction

IV. IMPULSE & ARTICULATION

Consonant	Function
P	Initiating impulse
B	Embodied impulse
F	Released / diffused impulse
D	Directed impact
G	Coagulated force

(P–B–F = classic male / female / child process cluster)

V. OPENING, CROSSING, LIMINALITY

Consonant   Function

J / Y Emergence / sprouting

L   Joining / linkage

Ḥ / X   Crossing / rupture

Q   Threshold decision

Z   Edge vibration / instability

VI. GOVERNANCE & MEASURE

Consonant   Function

Ṯ / Θ   Correct articulation

Š   Differentiation

Ḏ   Adjustment / tuning

TOTAL: 20 FUNCTIONAL CONSONANTS

If we count only primitives (no compounds like MT):

Ø, Ḥ, ⍰, M, T, K, W, N, S, R, P, B, F, D, G, J, L, Ḥ, Q, Z

= 20

Consonants were once actions. Alphabets are what happens when actions forget their source.

British **Museum number:** EA 589 Found in Malta, Ramesside period (19th Dynasty, time of Ramesses II)

On this small round-topped stela, Neferabu, a servant in the Place of Truth at Western Thebes, speaks across time with disarming clarity. He prays first to Ptah, Lord of Truth, king of the Two Lands, youthful of face and enthroned among the Ennead, asking not for power but for life, prosperity, health, intelligence, favour, and love, and for the grace that his eyes may behold Amun each day, as is granted to a righteous man who keeps the god within his heart. Turning the stone, his voice changes. He confesses openly that he once swore falsely by Ptah and was punished for it, made to see darkness in full daylight, reduced and exposed, likened to a stray in the street, marked by both men and gods. From this abasement, he draws his lesson and proclaims it aloud: Ptah does not overlook the deeds of any person, and his name must never be spoken falsely.

Inscriptions: In relief on both front and back, with hieroglyphic prayer texts to Ptah and reflections on divine justice.

Chapter 7 Ubuntu: A person is only a person through their relationship to others

Every inch within the Field of Dreams was a manifestation of perfection. The inner sanctum of the designers of the Centre was crafted with the finest qualities of the soul, so that their exteriors mirrored their inner artistic worlds. They treated stone and trees as sacred, much like our ancient ancestors did 7,000 years ago when they designed the world's oldest free-standing temples in Malta.

There is a certain light in all things that are dear or precious to us. We see light in beauty, gold, silver, pearls, and in everything that is pleasant.

An Ikebana arrangement in the centre of the room was whispering many secrets: the reds, golds, and oranges bathed us in warmth, luxury, and desire, while the blues and violets spread elegance, calmness, and reason. The asymmetry, commonly found in nature, presented us with informal, growing, wild aspects of life.

There were heavy and large flowers, bright and dark ones, strong and tall, curved and drooping, each one growing according to its own inherent rhythm. The colours of the flowers were in harmony with one another, and each had a special relationship with the container and the background of the room. Looking at them, I realised that they communicated with one another, giving each other space, pointing at each other, and showing the utmost respect to the centrepiece, the Queen of the bunch, which proudly stood out, admired by its siblings.

Different flowers convey different messages, and various countries have their own superstitions surrounding them. In Serbia, where I come from, for example, a blue flower is never given as a wedding gift because it is believed to bring 'bad luck'. The number of flowers must also be carefully counted: an even number for the cemetery and an odd number as a gift, given with good intentions.

The art of creating Ikebana can be traced back to a Buddhist monk who lived in the 15th century. Ikebana was his way of admiring and worshipping the beauty of nature.

Japanese Ikebana learnt from Zen its simplicity.

Elegant, natural, and refined, the subtle arrangement of rocks, flowers, shrubs, and running water gave me a sense of complete tranquillity.

To create an Ikebana arrangement, any part of the plant can be used – branches, leaves, grass, fruit.

Respecting nature's cycles, the monks valued withered leaves as highly as flowers in full bloom. In this peaceful art form, no movement was forced, no shape was perfect; nature was adored in its stunning asymmetry.

The silence and emptiness of the blossoms brought me to the Zen simplicity of the message: in order to reach the essence, we must respect the chaos, eliminate unnecessary movement, and dive into the unknown.

The first time I entered the Hypogeum, the Maltese underground shrine, I descended 11 meters to its core. Dancing barefoot in Kordin 3, a temple site usually closed to the public, I knew that our spiritual journey had begun millennia ago. The energy of the "Holy of Holies" enveloped me. As I spiraled deeper, a buzz within my ears confirmed the sacredness of this space. At the intersection of two paths in the Temple, I realized: God has no form—only the vibration of pure Consciousness. The place resonated strongly with this "Divine" energy.

I wrote:

John tells us:

"In the beginning was the Word, and the Word was with God, and the Word was God."

The Upanishads, sacred Hindu texts, say that the divine, all-encompassing consciousness first manifested as sound—OM—the vibration of the Supreme. Everything has its own frequency. Pythagoras, for instance, created a musical scale starting with the note A (just above middle C), resonating at 111 Hz. Perhaps this single note contains all the overtones, much like white light holds all colors. Perhaps it is a Cosmic "I love you," existing within all of us. Interestingly, 111 Hz is the frequency of a low male voice.

Professor Paul Devereux, an archaeo-acoustician from Cambridge, has studied ancient sites and temples, analyzing the ritual use of sound. He discovered that burial mounds in Ireland, called Cairns, though varying in materials and sizes, all resonate at a singular frequency: 111 Hz. Further studies showed that this frequency affects the brain in unique ways. MRI scans revealed that at precisely 111 Hz, the brain deactivates the prefrontal cortex—the center for language—and temporarily switches from left to right brain dominance, triggering intuitive, creative, and holistic processing. This induces a meditative or trance-like state.

Professor Robert Jahn's research into megalithic sites in the UK found similar acoustic behavior. These sites resonated between 95 and 120 Hz. The Maltese Hypogeum, a temple carved out of rock around 3600–2500 BC, mirrors the above-ground temples that are the world's oldest free-standing structures. Acoustic tests in the Oracle Chamber confirmed resonance at 111 Hz.

Seven thousand years ago, long before the Egyptian pyramids, an advanced and peaceful culture flourished in Malta, creating magnificent megalithic temples. There was no evidence of weapons or defensive architecture. Bone analyses suggest a healthy population. Their spiritual practices were life-affirming, attuned to the rhythms of the Earth, the Sun, and the Moon. They worshipped the Great Goddess, embodying both the feminine and the masculine divine.

These Neolithic people were far from primitive. They understood not only architecture but also sound rituals that induced altered states of consciousness. Such practices may have led individuals into trance-like meditations, increasing their emotional intelligence and social harmony.

Modern studies suggest that regular meditation can shape the brain, fostering patience, emotional balance, and creativity.

Descending into the Hypogeum, one reconnects with this ancient culture that employed overtone chanting, angelic singing, bell ringing, singing bowls, and drums to reach higher states of consciousness. These sacred rituals are found across world religions—Christian Mass singing, Tibetan and Buddhist chanting, Hindu devotional songs. The sound vibrated through the bones in the Hypogeum, and it is likely that pilgrims from around the known world came to Malta to experience these divine rites.

In the Hypogeum, researchers discovered dolichocephalous skulls: elongated skulls near a sacred well dedicated to the Mother Goddess, accompanied by a small statue of a sleeping goddess with a snake engraving. The snake, a symbol of wisdom, health, and esoteric knowledge, links these findings to ancient wisdom traditions.

When Saint Paul shipwrecked on Malta, he famously wrote of a snake biting his foot perhaps a final link to the island's serpent priesthood.

Fascinating, isn't it? A woman in her 50s, with a clear sense of purpose, excitedly shared her discoveries with me. She had been attending "psychic" workshops, honing her own abilities. "They've discovered a chamber full of paintings of spirits," she told me. "Their eyes are full of sparks, and they speak directly to your soul. You must see them!"

I found myself taken aback. Was it possible that we had become so distracted that we needed moving pictures to feel fulfilled?

It was Peter, Eileen, and Dorothy who had started this incredible project nearly forty years ago. In the beginning, they had nothing but a caravan and basic supplies, living on a barren, sandy plot of land. The locals warned them that the soil was unfit for farming, that it would never bear fruit. Yet, these three dreamers forged ahead, growing the largest vegetables anyone had ever seen, turning the land into something miraculous through sheer determination and years of composting.

Soon, the place was transformed into a thriving eco-village, complete with caravans, eco-houses, and workshops. It was a community entirely self-sufficient in water and energy, where everything, every decision and every action, was done with care and consciousness. I could hear their discussions as I walked through the Field of Dreams: questions about the best colour for a fence, whether it would blend with the landscape, how to honour the arts, where to place the meditation sanctuary.

Their water was purified using a highly sophisticated biological sewage treatment plant, which doubled as a botanical garden. The plants filtered the water naturally, embodying the interconnectedness of all things. It was a beautiful, living testament to their dedication and love for the planet.

The creation of this sanctuary had been a long and sometimes tumultuous process: disagreements, delays, and decisions made on divine inspiration. But through it all, they remained steadfast in their vision. They navigated challenges just as we all do, with patience, wisdom, and an unwavering sense of purpose.

As I walked through the Field, I couldn't help but reflect on my own journey. I thought of Rudolf, a lawyer who had single-handedly reforested the north of Malta, turning barren clay into a flourishing national park. I had collaborated with his NGO, Gaia, to organize six Body, Mind, and Spirit festivals. It began with 100 attendees and grew to over 3,000.

That night, as we talked beneath the stars, I drifted into sleep with thoughts of creatures in the woods, taking me on a journey through the Milky Way and back, gifting me with the sensation of disappearing—of simply Being.

The next day, as I wandered through the Field, I met Stephie, a German-speaking woman. She shared with me a recurring dream she had: "I feel as though I am surrounded by an eggshell. It's fragile, and I just need to concentrate deeply to break through it. On the other side, I know there will be light and life waiting."

I asked, "Have you ever tried to break through the shell in your dream?"

She smiled thoughtfully. "Metaphysically?"

"Literally," I replied.

"I'll try," she said, and we parted ways.

The next day, she found me and excitedly told me about her experience. "At first, I couldn't find a way out. But then I shifted my position, focused, and cracked the shell open. I grew bigger, becoming a star. We were all energy, pulsating together. It was beautiful."

Her eyes shimmered with excitement as she shared her transformation. "What's your imagery?" she asked.

I hesitated, then spoke from the heart: "A Bedouin in the desert, questioning the meaning of life. A traveler through time who refuses to anchor, a shadow on the wall that depends on light."

Stephie was silent for a moment, then asked, "Will your inner core ever tire of this search?"

"Silence," I whispered, feeling the depth of the moment. "Experience silence."

As I stood there in the BliSS, Silence carried Internal Union, the alchemy of the soul. The alchemy of love. The alchemy of Humanity.Silence carried Sat Chit Ananda.

sintIn China only the ruling class could wear red for 1,000s of years.

Like with guerrilla, soldiers, a political party, or a large company, within an Ashram one is asked to take off the old clothes, forget old friends, family, customs. Following a strenuous daily routine with a lack of sleep and privacy one starts building the relationship with the guru, or the Boss.

In no time the life stage becomes so overpowering that the soul forgets that it had ever existed before the moment of entering into a camp. The 'I's shed off their skins, one by one, staying naked, exposed to the supreme ideology or the leader, always carefully marked within yearly personal reviews.

> You should find your Guru. Not challenge him but trust him and give yourself completely. That is when you are going to feel his divine grace...

At the other side of the world, Sai Baba performed his-own set of miracles. He got famous for materializing gold. A golden egg or a ring spit out in the midst of spiritual gatherings... 1,000s of followers flocked to receive a spiritual gift and guidelines. During the purification, holy dust had materialized on the top of his paintings. His speeches were often interrupted by delirious screams of disciples entering into unconscious adoration trances.

> The guru is a manifestation of Divine. He is the supreme one, He is Divine. He dispels darkness and brings light into souls. Another sentence that follows the aura of the chosen One.

Following this definition, a difficult mission for any soul to fulfill, Guru just could not be wrong. A bit like our Holy Scripts that were divine and could not be questioned. Thousands of synchronicities get woven into the fabric of a Guru making. The techniques are many, tried and tested during 1,000s of years, so now the top marketing Gurus of various politicians and show-business personalities execute the same.

It all had started with the motion that mortals are insignificant. Millions of worthless souls, in need to go into the pot called "special".

To "earn" the status we pass through an "initiation", or "baptism", or "promotion", uniting him (since it was always him) with Holy Spirit or secrets of Kundalini opening, or the Board of Directors.

Until recently, surrounded by sickness and poverty, feeding hungry mouths was a major goal in any of the family on our little planet.

Educating a child within the Government or Church, had sometimes created highly respected personalities, promoting the scholars who wrote books, into the category of "saints".

Still the motion of the "special" ones kept the Earth turning. The richer sons from the Colonial countries, had been educated, gifting them with the aura of superiority.

Having a private doctor, meant one can also sustain a household full of servants, friends, teachers, artists, employees...

The commodity of free schooling and health, had become our reality just very recently.

The King showered grace. Closer to the King, closer to the source of power. The King was so isolated in China that he could not exit the Royal City. Imagine this, you cannot exit your golden prison, always followed by thousands! Does this remind you of our show-business Divas? Whether an Elvis or a Monro, the path is the one of the enchantment of the crowds.

Practicing mysticism or magic, for example Kabbalah, or Hinduist Yoga with its prayers, mantras, colours, angels hierarchies, large industries are now manipulating tools, emotionally black-mailing millions of kids, the way Hitler had done, using ancient symbols, sounds (GooGLe = GoD), so that our mental set-up, psychological response mechanisms, resonate with: BuY.

So, where do we draw the line?

Materialized in the body of a chimpanzee, with words "VITRIOL" written on his forehead, a soul of a man, once Alchemist, finding himself within these karmic circumstances can testify we are all confused.

Both Muslims and Hindus insist that the union with God should stay our daily encounter. In his practices, a Zen Buddhist will enter silence. Within a Christian mysticism, this silent encounter with Divine is within our relationship to art or music.

Within the scientific observations of different types of atoms at similar energy levels, the states with the similar behaviour patterns are called: solid, liquid, gas, and plasma.

This classification is from the Ancient Greek system of Aristotle, who was born in 387 BC in Athens, to the outside world better known as the teacher, advisor, & consultant of the Government.

The Greek Parthenon is an ancient temple on the Athenian Acropolis in Greece, dedicated to the goddess Athena. Built in 450 BC, during the height of the Athenian Empire, it was a marvel of its time. Yet, during the early 1800s, Lord Elgin, the British ambassador to the Ottoman Empire — who was occupying Christian Greece at the time — removed about half of the temple and transported it to Britain. The ancient Greek treasure now sits on display in the British Museum in London, alongside the full set of Egyptian mummies taken from Egypt. Since the early 1980s, Greek governments have disputed the British Museum's legal title to these priceless sculptures.

"What a tragedy," I said to my guide, standing before the half-exposed relics. "How much has been taken from this place. The spirit of it... how does it feel, to witness something so ancient, so stolen?"

The guide, an older man with graying hair and wise eyes, looked out over the ruins, his voice heavy with a quiet grief. "It feels as though history itself is mourning. The Parthenon is not just stones and columns. It is a symbol, a vessel of culture. To see it stripped — well, that leaves an emptiness that can never quite be filled."

"What do the spirits say?" I asked, half-joking, but still sincere in my curiosity. "The ones who lived here, who worshipped Athena."

He smiled faintly. "They whisper. If you listen close enough, on the wind or through the creak of the old stone, you might hear them, speaking of times long gone.. "

I paused, feeling the weight of his words settle in, and then asked, "And is it true? Was there a temple here long before the Parthenon?"

His gaze turned thoughtful, distant. "Yes. The Neolithic remains found on the Acropolis indicate a temple existed here as far back as 2,800 BC. And in a way, it is as if the land remembers... even when the stones forget.

Later, in the heart of Kathmandu, within the Himalayan Buddhist Meditation Centre, I met a monk who had been meditating for decades. As we sat together on the floor of the simple room, he spoke of the nature of the mind.

"You come here seeking peace," he said, his voice gentle but penetrating."

I nodded, recalling the months of chanting prayers, the long days filled with meditation. "How do you find peace?" I asked. "The worries that burden us every day?"

He smiled, closing his eyes as though in deep thought. "By understanding that all is impermanent. Your suffering, your joy, both are fleeting. To cling to them is to invite suffering. Instead, embrace them as they are, and then let them pass."

I sat in silence, contemplating his words, feeling as though a veil had lifted, if only for a moment.

Months later, in New Zealand, I found myself at an Ananda Marga Ashram in Auckland, helping Dada with his Jet Boat Pegasus. One afternoon, after a long session of meditation, I asked him, "How do you balance the work of the mind and the work of the body? How do you find harmony between them?"

Dada laughed softly, his eyes twinkling with quiet amusement. "You don't. Not in the way you think. The mind wants control, but the body only knows surrender. You listen. You listen to the small, subtle things

— the breath, the movement of energy. The body knows much more than we realize, but we've learned to ignore it."

In Spain, during my month-long Sivananda Yoga Teacher Training, the days were long and demanding. After one particularly grueling session, I asked my instructor, "Why do we push ourselves so hard in our practice? Isn't there a balance between effort and ease?"

She looked at me, her face calm, as though she had anticipated the question. "The challenge is not to perform perfectly, but to surrender to the practice, to the breath. When you surrender fully, you will find that ease follows."

Her words stayed with me, as did the lessons of the many places I visited, each teaching me something new about consciousness. Yet, it was only later, when reflecting on my family's history, that I truly grasped the meaning of surrender.

My father's mother had died of cancer, leaving five young children. Their world was shattered in an instant.

"She was the heart of the family," my aunt once told me. "And when she was gone... everything crumbled."

The children were scattered, sent from cousins to institutions, until my father grew old enough to bring them under his care. They never spoke the word "cancer," not in the way we know it.

"Is it Him?" He asked his mother one night, looking at her as she stood by the window, staring out into the dark sky.

"Him," my mother muttered, her voice low, heavy with grief. "Let the devil take him. Him, for Christ's sake."

In our family, we carried the weight of Him — it is in our DNAs, the very essence of Death. It bound us together, in a strange, unspoken way.

The compassion I felt during my travels deepened in me, especially after visiting the slums of Addis Ababa. Working with Sister Ludgarda, a Maltese nun in her 60s, was both humbling and heartbreaking. She cared for 150 children, many of whom were HIV-positive, orphans, and deeply in need.

One afternoon, as we stood together outside the orphanage, I asked her, "How do you keep going? How do you not break under the weight of it all?"

She smiled, but it wasn't the smile of someone who had the answers. "I hold the babies," she said. "I make sure that each one of 150 of them is held with love. I love, because love gives."

Her words echoed through me. It was not just about surviving, but about loving.

And perhaps, as my father once said, "The more we connect, the more we understand the meaning of what it means to live." My father's mother died of cancer, leaving five children, the youngest just two years old. Her husband soon followed her into the world of Death, transforming a once-happy family into a brood of orphans.

"We had everything," my aunt recalls, "and now we could no longer ask for milk in our white coffee."

Coming from war-stricken countries has a similar effect on some of us. My visit to Africa and Asia swept me out of my small puddle of existence and into the ocean of compassion, breaking through my limitations.

"Well," I said, leaning back in my chair, "whenever I hear someone moaning about their day-to-day problems, I always think, 'You need a dose of perspective.' I tell them to go to Addis Abeba, to the slums there, and spend a couple of weeks helping out Sister Ludgarda at her orphanage."

"Sister Ludgarda?" my friend asked, leaning in slightly, intrigued.

"Yes," I nodded. "She's a Maltese nun. Over sixty now, but she's been running this orphanage for years. In one of the poorest places in the world, she manages the care of around 150 children, many of them with HIV. She's got a lot on her plate, to say the least."

"Goodness, that sounds like an awful lot for one person," my friend murmured, clearly struck by the thought.

"It is," I agreed, "but somehow, she makes it work. I've seen her go out in her old van, driving across town to take babies to the hospital, picking up medicine for sick children, or going to adoption hearings. Even though she's burdened with age and illness herself, she doesn't slow down. And still — despite everything — she always finds a way to give. I've seen her fill her pockets with sweets to give to the little ones begging in the streets."

My friend stared at me, wide-eyed. "How sweet…."

"I know," I said quietly, nodding. "It's a kind of awareness I've never really seen before. To keep giving, even when you're exhausted, when you're physically unwell. It makes you realize that some of the things we think are struggles… well, they're nothing in comparison."

"Wow," my friend whispered. "the truth is, half of the humankind lives in very poor conditions.."

"It really is," I said, a small smile tugging at my lips. "It makes everything else feel so insignificant, doesn't it? It's hard to complain about anything again."

As a member of a family, a group, a country, as a woman with white skin, while within the orphanage, I was on the brink of something entirely new.

As a yoga teacher, as a poet, as a writer, as a manager, I still could not fully connect with compassion. But as a mother, the understanding of this quality became more profound. Praying for the health of each baby fortunate enough to still be breathing, I felt compassion for all.

In the midst of all this, I met Dattatreya — a man whose physical presence was striking, whose wisdom was more profound than my own. One day, I asked him, "Do you feel detached from the world of senses?"

"No," he replied, "I am still working on it."

I felt a deep, instant attraction to him. There was something magnetic about his being, a powerful energy I longed to embrace. But, as we spent time together, meditating, practicing yoga, and sharing mantras, I began to question the very nature of love and attachment. Was it wise to renounce our senses, to deny the pleasures of the physical world, in pursuit of a higher truth?

One evening, as our eyes met across a crowded room, I wrote:

Scorpion Sting

Fascinated by the frames,

Absorbed in the reality of many,

Stung by the scorpion sting,

Paralyzed,

Freezing images that are fluid,

Measuring, Defining,

Arresting the infinite within the finite,

Perceiving, Believing, Squaring the circle,

Attached to the illusion of constant change and separation.

children with me?" his answer was still no. I wrote:

Truth Hidden in a Handshake

She touched my hands — hers were cold, trembling.

"Please tell us if we can help you in any way," she said.

She spoke of her love for him, her insecurity, but we both knew — without speaking the words — that we shared a common understanding. He was a rare bird — monogamous, locked within a golden windowpane. He had given up on love.

And I wrote –

THE VOICE OF DIS-APPEARANCE

I hear the voice from the centre of the earth
your image hallucination takes over me
organic, orgasmic, organoid

who are you Mr. Sadness - have we met before?

I look at my fingers, keyboard, the vase on my desk, trying not to cry
but it is all in vain - the night is taking over
the music of dis-appearance

You have dis-appeared before we have truly met
gone under the cover: hidden within the nothingness
leaving with me images of love and trust and peace

Chirping outside our window was a parrot, or was it the heater that
cheated the noise
unearthly, profound, mystical, real was your smell

I found you and lost you within the same thought
Did you know: Love comes with the surrender that is greater than
your-Self

I see us holding hands, chatting aimlessly
Lying on the sofa covered with moments of nakedness
I will have my coffee in the morning in Ole as usual
and you will have yours in Rome

I have met you, against all odds of the Universe that likes playing jokes
on us mortals
and lost you before we have truly met.

Chapter 8 Spiral

A shell in the form of a stone — or perhaps a stone in the form of a shell — found me.

Once, Earth was wise. Humans lived in harmony with spirits, animals, and plants. Understanding the spiral's path was not so elusive. The dead were consulted for guidance, and all stages of life and death were honored. It was not so difficult, thousands of years ago, to go to the very core of Being.

The core of life, at the center of the spiral, still holds the secret of the beginning of creation. This ancient wisdom is known to shells, to DNA, to constellations, and like a battery connecting to its source, life connects to the sun. Breathing returns to its source within Gaia, weaving through her intricate web of causes and effects.

In the spiritual narrative of our souls, everything can be seen as a clue or a guiding step forward.

When we look at each other, a miracle happens — he said — we fall in love. A soul opens to another, and we fall in love. We learn to keep our gaze brief,

Down to the ground, communicating what must be said with deep eye contact. Losing boundaries, we abandon pretense, expectations, and stay with pure soul experiences. After a sacred silence, he added:

> This dance is our divine appointment, and no one is here by accident.

Conscious Love

Love under Will

Instinctive Love

Falling in Love

Love as Divine Flow

Love-Head-Aches

Love-Sex Frustrations

Love-Karmic Patterns

Mysterious, untouchable Venus—veiled and desired—

Our endless hunger for her beauty...

To remove her from her shell,

Imprison her in the woods of our love-thirsty subconscious
darkness—

To possess her, to tear her into shreds,

Desiring her purity, her sight, her light,

Disappearing into her being,

Dissolving, merging, creating,

As Gods would...

Love for the sane, in a moment of self-inflicted madness,

Becomes love for the insane.

Yet how deeply we long for this insanity.

The first kiss

Becomes love for the too-experienced,

And within its rawness, hides the secret of its beginnings.

Can love stay virginal?

Can we keep it alive in our stomachs, hearts, knees—

Trembling,

Like the desperate passion of an 18-year-old,

Soaked in first-time love?

Can we keep it unstained

By jealousy, possessiveness, pride,

And still harvest its fruits,

Even when they are attacked

By the spiders of decay, netted in the webs of boredom?

Can it be full, eternal, all-giving, ego-demolishing?

Can we stay obsessed

Yet detached?

And, last but not least...

Can we leave at any time,

Because our drive towards the Divine

Is always a little bit stronger?

Chapter 9 Wu Wei

flow of Life governed by Tao
　　　　　flow of change

spontaneous
　　natural
　　　　effortless
　　　　　　acting through non-action

connecting with Earth and Moon and Sun
through
being

not inert or lazy or passive
　　but swimming swiftly
　　　　within the current
　　　　　　merging Life with Tao

quiet and watchful
not-interfering
receptive
alert
directly **connected**

acting　　　　without　action
　　trusting　detached　without desire
spontaneous　natural　　　effortless
　　　　Living

Love is the strongest feeling I have ever experienced and the death of
love was very hard to handle. Entering love as a divine source, opens
our drive towards eternal love offering this comforting thought that we
are never really alone.

At this most magical of places, we performed the 4 Elements Wedding Ritual. At the table, we gathered four symbols, placing them in accordance with the 4 Directions. Air, as East, as Yellow, as the Rising Sun, as Birth, was represented by an eagle feather and air purified with incense (we used Nag Champa). We offered our respect to the stage of Birth, asking Sages and Saints to support the birth of good and fruitful initiatives.

My son played a flute, creating the magic sound of AIR. Fire, as South, as Red, as Life Force, was manifested within the lit candles. Fire, in its highest manifestation, is Divine Love. We asked the Angels to guide our Life Force towards Divine Love. Water, as West, as Dark Blue, as Emotions, as the Setting Sun, was mixed with Jasmine, Rose, and Lavender. Passing the vessels around, people gave their blessings. Water, in its highest manifestation, is Peace. We asked the Ancestors to guide us towards Peace.

Earth, as North, as White, as Winter, as the Wisdom of Elders, was represented by sacred stones. One of them, chosen for its colour and beauty, became the symbol of Earth. The highest manifestation of Earth energies is the Land of Plenty. We asked Scientists to help us live within the World of Plenty. We also gave our respect to the central force, the force that unites all the elements into Tao, the Life Flow, represented by Green. A green branch was passed along to symbolise Life. Passing the branch, the couple made their vows to each other. Passing the branch, the honoured guests gave their blessings.

Together, we repeated: "Mother of Form and the Father of Consciousness Unite within this Sacred Marriage." The couple kissed, the participants surrounded them in a Universal Hug, and all sang AUM.

Finding the words to describe this magical ceremony that took place at the Equinox, this poem came to me...

Taking steps in trust, child-full playfulness and joyful peace
    Chanting, drumming, humming, dancing at the most Sacred Palace
    Resonating with the Song of Life
    We touched the Spiral where Forest meets Rivers
    Ascending the deepest caves where Stalactites and Stalagmites
    form Castles

Of Eternal Lovers meditating within the Earth's Belly

Mirroring What is Below is Above
We were 12 Honorable Guests witnessing the Sacred Marriage

The Mother of Form united with the Father of Consciousness

Asking Sages, Saints to give our Initiatives Fruitfulness
Angels to protect our Fire of Life
Ancestors to guard our Wisdom
Scientists to guide us towards the Land of Plenty

Holding each other's space, souls' expression, laughter
We honored the 4 elements letting the Equinox
Flow through the Spiral of our DNAs

Worshiping the Central Force that unites us with the Universe
Becoming a Vessel of Love that is Life
We merged with Tao.

During the 10-day spiritual wedding, we "camped" together in the attic of a small guest house that hosted the event. Ten of us would eat, meditate, walk, dance, create rituals, and discuss various aspects of relationships.

At the spiritual marriage of Bani and Rob, some 10 years later, there were no priests, my kids took them from one side of the forest to the other, with no vows they looked at each other's eyes and expressed their souls wish to unite in harmony living within a Marriage that is not of eternal love but of truthfulness and trust within a conscious relationship.

At the wedding ceremony, in Czech Republic, we gathered at the Moravian Karst, a protected nature reserve, with 100 km² of pristine countryside. Our cottage was just on the top of a matrix of caves where Punkva river slept in its abode.

Located at the edge of virtually vertical cliff that formed the Macocha

Abyss with its entrance to the most sacred cave that hid huge millions of years old stalagmites, stalactites, with stalactite curtains and cascades all resembling a dance of underground ferries. Punkva Caves were discovered in 1723 and they were open to public in 1910, only a hundred of years ago, when we (humanity) got electricity. Under a tree, with all of us dressed in white, I gave my Blessing to the Couple:

> We gathered here to acknowledge and deepen the soul-mate union of these two lovely souls. We are here to support this amazing Twin Flame honoring the Bounty of Life. May you take steps in trust holding each other through all of your vulnerabilities and learnings, co-creating Life together, opening deeper towards Love, Love that is Wild, Love that is Still. May Angels give you Wisdom to cherish, nurture, and respect one another, choosing trust and honesty above All. May God give you Strength to resonate with the Song of Life fully honoring the truth of each other. Mother of Form and the Father of Consciousness Unite within this Sacred Marriage!

The spiral kept reappearing in my life.

All my research into Goddess worship, the ancient megalithic sites, the Maltese temples — Each stamped by the spiral.

This mystical, magical symbol became the centerpiece of Bani and Rob's spiritual wedding,

Tattooed on our feet, hands, and faces,

Pinned in our hair, carried as thought-forms within our speech.

Receiving a talking branch just before the ceremony, beneath the trees in the Czech Republic,

Conducted by my two children, all dressed in white,

I expressed:

142

It is the dot that wishes to manifest as an infinite end; the endless expansion that occurs throughout nature. It is 'I' that becomes 'All,' the Hindu 'So-Ham' (I am It), representing our union with God, the circle.

An altar filled with candles and offerings smiled at us: flower petals, grains of sand, dried grass, and other magical substances. In silence, she offered an invocation to the Divine, blowing the four-element mixture into the audience. From that moment, we were under a spell.

"This is the astrological story of now," I said, "and we will connect it to our path. Our ancestors' tales repeat, creating patterns that haunt us. To stop them from reappearing, we must excavate them — rediscovering, reopening, redoing their beginnings and endings."

Venus dances her universal dance with Jupiter in Leo, Mercury retraces his steps through Scorpio, and Uranus and Neptune conspire in laughter. What if we can break the pattern? birds asked. What if we deliberately break the patterns established since the beginning of time? Do you believe in reincarnation?

"What drives people to war with themselves is the suspicion— or the knowledge — that they consist of two opposing persons... the conflict may be between the sensual and spiritual self, or between the ego and the shadow," said Jung.

And so I wrote:

Ouroboros

When I heard their message for the third time,

I knew my moment had come — for initiation.

I lay on a bed of flowers, surrounded by the sound of chimes,

And I gave him the key to the temple of Truth.

In the center of the belly, I met Her — Amaru,

The Serpent Path of the South.

I dove into her waters and watched her shed her skin,

Transforming wounds into sources of power,

Giving Earth Life, and me Fluidity.

I met Otorongo within my heart,

Stepping onto the Jaguar Path of the West.

I followed her effortless run

Through woods, air, and waters,

Cuddling the fearless cat to learn Courage, Strength, and Love.

I climbed the mountain in my mind

To become One with Apuchin — the Eagle Path of the East.

I flew, dissolved within the light,

Knowing that there is no more

To do, to be, nowhere to go.

Dreaming the world into being, visions into realities.

Exiting the flight, coming back to Earth, I noticed

My skin was gold, transcendent.

My mind was luminous, emotions gentle,

Ready to begin the path of The Fool,

Prepared to experience the Serpent swallow its tail,

Secure in God's emotional embrace — meditating.

Karen Blixen: "It takes terrible courage to create"

Dreams

The Bigger
The more Imaginative
The more Limitless
Our Dreams are
Closer we are
To Him

LIKE THE SEA BEFORE THE STORM

with his head against my chest
fragile and beautiful, my baby-boy was sick

his solemn, tranquil eyes reminded me of:

poppy's red delicate petals
in the middle of the Maltese gorge

of butterfly's wings
against the 1000 years old stone fortress

of albatrosses' feathers
in the middle of the rough sea

of the texture of the spider's web
in the deserted house, not open for ages

of the breath of the sea-horse
moaning for his loved one who was killed last night

of a cat just giving a birth
to her first ever kitten

of Buddha's 101-st hour
under the tree where he got enlightened

yesterday, my baby-boy was sick,

gentle, sensitive, weak
he reminded me of the energy of the sea - just before the storm

LOVE'S CLAWS AND SPERM WHALE VOMIT

You know you have been caught by the love's claws when:

You are a black widow spider's mate
And you enter her net willingly even though
Your mum, TV, and neighbors, have warned you not to

You are a fish that follows the loved one into the fisherman net
Praying your head hits the hull next to hers

You search the world for the sperm whale vomit
So that you can put it into the essential oils
He could smell - with the scents of your skin

You listen to the radio as though it is for the first time
and hear your story in every single song
That sings of love or pain or longing

You clearly feel the wound bleeding
But testosterone and oxytocin in the blood are raising
And your heart's bit hits the record when he stands next to you

When chance, Faith, circumstances, Universe say NO
And you ignore it, listening to his voice on the other end
With a shiver causing a storm on the other side of Atlantic

TRUST OR PIXIE DUST

Woven in silence
your refusal to let me in

Golden leaves cover the surface of your body
inch by inch
I re-discover it within mine

Re-incarnated through our troubles
your thoughts scattered on the floor
covered in the full moon shadow

Is Sorrow your name
or Joy or Trust or
Pixie Dust
Like rice paper or poppy's petals
fragile and soft
your tears mix with mine

Come closer, my love, close enough so I'll feel your breath
that is where the key-hole hides
in your breath and in the centre of your palm

Come closer, my love, together we could hope to find
the code
that breaks the lock that separates your soul from mine

FALLING-IN-LOVE

Sharp and vibrant
your eyes
move me into this familiar feeling
of being connected

Starkly and volatile
swirling through my heart
is the virus that merges
your aura with mine

I cling to your promises
of softness and peace
and take a chance in a million
to let you in

Trusting and trussing

the images on the mirror of our souls

manifesting us
in the future of our thoughts

I believe in you within me
Can you believe in me within you?

Come closer, my love, together we could hope to find
the code
that breaks the lock that separates your soul from mine

PHATAMORGANA

A hurricane on the horizon...
Do you understand the difference?
Destroying the other – acting merciless, human-less, life-less
Little droplets became an ice-storm
To get me established onto the path of the Fool
Unmoved, untouched, inspired
No frost-bites can tease me out of this peace
The winds chase the ghosts
Into my mind, into my life, into my heart
And yet I still believe in Love
In this oasis within the dessert depths
Sure - it is a phatamorgana

And sure - it is the one I want to believe in...

Silence

There is silence within us that is more powerful than any thought,
and as water is stronger than the strongest stone,
so is its Wisdom,
that creates without efforts and moves without movements
that gives without limits when you open the Doors of Being.
Step in it living Trust and you will Know It!

TO GANDHI

I hear the calling
- to become schism, to rebel, contract
to all that is NOT real
and give a chance to
mermaids, fairies, goblins
of our past lives and the in-born rights
- to hummer
into our brain waves
a golden thread
of NON-VIOLENCE
that is so hard to comprehend

A Miracle

This morning I sprinkled love on my cereals
& a miracle happened!
Sun smiled at me from behind the clouds
Sea changed its colour to deep coral blue
Wind whispered secrets in my ear
& people started moving slooowly
As though they are enchanted...

VULNERABILITY

It's place is not at the beginning
but at the very end of the journey of love

If we feel it at the very beginning of the relationship
we have mistaken it for fear...

who is the one you ask for forgiveness
when Life knocks at your door
and you pretend that you are not at home?

SAT-CHIT-ANANDA

A kiss of primordial Self
within the sat-chit-ananada
in the centre of a thousand petalled lotus
Being
giving & receiving
Life
breathing the nature of Para Brahman
experiencing

existence-consciousness-bliss

OROBOUROS

When I heard their message for the third time
I knew that my moment has come - for an initiation
Lying on a bed of flowers, surrounded by the sound of chimes I gave
him the key to the Temple of Truth

In the centre of the belly was Her: Amaru
The Serpent Path of the South
I dived into her waters and watch her shed her skin
Transforming wounds into sources of power
Giving Earth - Life, and me - Fluidity

Within my heart I met Otorongo
Stepping into the Jaguar Path of the West
Following her effortless run through woods, air, waters
I cuddled fearless cat to learn Courage, Strength & Love

Climbing mountains within my head to become One with Apuchin -
the Eagle Path of the East
Dissolved within the Light Knowing there is no-more

Dreaming the World into Being, Visions into Realities
Exiting the flight, coming back to Earth, I noticed
My skin was gold, transcendent
My mind was luminous, emotions gentle

Prepared to start the path of The Fool
Ready to experience the Serpent swallow its tail
The Kingdom is in the Heart of One and All where
One IS All and All IS One
The One can rest

VAJRAYANA - THE DIAMOND TRUTH

I will give this Sermon Naked
Like St Francis once did
A jongleur for God
An inspiring holy madman
With the knowledge that
Only NAKED IS true

I will raise this cup
For Vajrayana – the diamond truth
Where thunderbolt unites with lotus
Upaya with Prajna

Ida with Pingala

Yin with Yang
Vratyas & Dakinis will dance their sacred dance
United with Shakti,

Shiva will whisper

Into her ear
The secret of **Eternal Bliss**

NOTHINGNESS

Embedded within rocks
Hidden amongst star clusters
Your Holy Presence is so close to mine

Like in a dream, I see You
Even though
You are Not

I hear You within the silence
Touching the spiral of Life & Death

I bow my head in respect &
I feel You bow Yours to mine

One amongst the thousand of corpses
One amongst the thousand of new-borns

Here
Within Your Kingdom
I stay

RHYTHM OF AFRICA

Rhythm of Africa
Call of the Motherland
Rooted inside of each-one-of-us

To be truthful to our Purpose
To be truthful to our Ancestors
To the essence of Holy of Holiest
To the shriek of the centre of the Earth
To our connection with the great Ones

Divine Light as pouring vortex
Enters the djembe beats
Attuning with the pulse of the Universe
Transforming Chaos into a well defined Pattern and
The well defined Pattern into the Chaos

I know that the sky Awaits
and today I celebrate

Her Majesty: the Flight

SOHAM

Watching passing images
listening to the sounds
i feel attached to the sense of Beauty
i feel detached of the sense of 'I'

-'I' that is my mind
-'I' that are my feelings
-'I' that are my words or my looks

I feel closer to the 'i' that is SOHAM
that is OM MANE PADME HUM
that is SAT CHIT ANANDA
that exist in NON-existence
that breaths through NON-breathing
and connects to Essence that is Being
that knows no beginnings nor ends

footprints in the snow of time
undiscovered by Saturn's insight-full torch
karma's cloud colors the Soul
healing love's bites meet the magic light

when a particle and antiparticle touch
they both disappear in a burst
of gamma radiation
that generates huge amount of energy.
Can this be love?

THELMA AND AGAPE

Will and Love - practiced
to invoke her Majesty **Kundalini**
In the world where adepts die and bloom as Lotuses
The perfection of Union is **Silence**

The desire for Beauty within a **Dolphin**
that possesses the Soul
keeping it under the **Abyss** - giving It the Madness of Pan
seeking the totality of all possible 'do'-s
jumping into the river full of streams of thoughts

Until...

The steady sound of **Harph** stills Its mind
freeing it from its grossness and violence
destroying the illusions of shame and desires,
and loathsome forms of ego-structures
allowing **Faun** to appear and accept Its True Nature

Aiming at **Perfection** - day after day
Purging all of 'I's - uniting with 'All'
the Will finally becomes the Self
the Faun transforms into the **Unicorn**
that knows the life of pure joy
and have only thoughts of clarity and splendor

Worshiping Silence - Ecstasy Transcends Expression
The Soul is **Freed**

Can the magic be a life style?
Maya can...

GRATITUDE

Crystal clear is my mind
Sound of Aum within my silence
Subtly-constantly-opening
To Divine Light
To Divine Wisdom,
To Divine Flow,
With the strong Gratitude
That I am where I am

Celebrating your uniqueness
respecting your Might
I'll give myself to you
through starry nights

SPIRAL

What happens to decisions
discoveries, pathways that
spiral through our lives

Where are they hidden?

Can we hit the centre
whirl-pooling through the universe
using
the circle of emotions
of guesses,
of little or no knowledge
of someone's else's images
seen on TV
of hands
that make the same mistake
without learning
of the lunatics
burning in rectifying fire
of love that knows no way
of a man that could not move
attached to a cock of power
miraculously awakened, attuned,
shaken
leaving everything behind
screaming screams that can not
be heard - only sensed

ONE IN A BILLION

Thousands will come to your rescue
And you will enquire and merge and divide
until no more cells are left to multiply
until no more hope is left to clarify
Your search

Bugs feed by sucking fluids from
other beings - only few are harmful
Some species suck blood - only few kill
You will seek and learn
that you are not even one
in a billion

I give respect to you – my silent warrior
who fight for love with all his might
I give respect to your heart's echoes
your call is so very precious...

NISHAGHANDHI

A rock looms of my gloom
a distant sound of AUM becomes
louder and louder

A plunging gorge opens as a pearl
One step and we will reach eternity: in a second

Hold on the mighty one
hold on to your mother's skirt

You stumble across planes
leaving a bloody trail behind you

Hold on the mighty one
and in time before your death
you might discover the cave
carved from tears
by the Holy Men
from all over the world
night-after-night
day-after-day
in prayer

WU WEI

flow of Life governed by Tao
            flow of change

spontaneous
        natural
            effortless
                    acting through non-action

connecting with Earth and Moon and Sun
through
being

not inert or lazy or passive
        but swimming swiftly
                within the current
                        merging Life with Tao

quiet and watchful
not-interfering
receptive
alert
directly **connected**

acting   without   action
        trusting   detached without desire
spontaneous   natural   effortless
                                Living

WHERE NO TIME EXISTS

i jumped into the centre
of the spiral
enchanted - i followed
and found myself
inside the centre of Being

will you join me?

AND SHE SAID...

Dive into the center of a spiral,
expand beyond its edge becoming eternal
Dance with your lover
and dream your truth laughing in ecstasy

'For I am divided for love's sake, for the chance of union.'

'Invoke me under my stars! Love is the law, love under will.'

Arise, come forth, and live and
I will give you unimaginable joy...

HARP'S SOUNDS FOLLOWED ME

Was it avalanche that stopped me or a hurricane?
from reaching out for your hands
covering my soul with the golden dust

into the centre of the spiral
into the essence of the pentagram
into the light of a rainbow
into the tear of the newborn
into the stem of the rose

SoHaM

AWAKENING

I woke up with a thought - do you remember?

A feather on my lap and
a tickle at the bottom of the pond of memories
buried a sound of a deserted beach
I returned...

Opening my eyes once again, I whispered - is this a mistake?

An error on the page kept bouncing back
could not handle the failure of its own reflection
within the mirror of constant movement

I let them come-in and stayed puzzled with the noises - madness?

In an instant
100s of faces crammed within the same story
Move away - I shrugged them off
I need some air!

I looked around me and found nothing but zero-ness

Wall covered with golden leaves
stopped me on the way to Hell
I piled them off one by one
discovering layers of nothingness
filled with space and the sound of AUM

And I closed my eyes to dissolve within its cure

INITIATION TIME

Just there behind the curtain
It was surreal, strange and cunning
full of blood and action, underground screams
demanding attention
demanding space
within the show of puppets on the stage

I saw them clearly, all gathered together,
for a perfect set-up

Kali and Shakti, Gaia and Tara
de-sce-nded
to give us - mortals, followers, martins

Some...   Initiation time

Some...   Magic of forms and sounds

Some...   Whispers from within the earth

Some...   Intimate knowledge and

A possibility

To completely understand

Her Sacred Path

PRIVILEGED TO BE THERE

We walked through the labyrinth
In search of the sacred stone within our hearts
Holding hands - we sang and celebrated Life
We descended deep into the Oracle hole
Humming Aum with didgeridoo
We got lost in each others' eyes – many, many times
All of us – worshipers of Her Might
We entered Her channels
To learn & to experience to Be
All became One for a very brief moment
That will stay with us – for eternity
Of sacredness, of holiness, of bliss

The tree stood silent and barren
A man provoked me
I could not hear the sound of the rain
Was too obsessed with the notion of Self

IN SEARCH OF THE HIGHEST

Magic world within imagination - catch me - descending

Searching for the highest you eventually bump into God

Until then...
stay
the most perfect
the most understanding
the most unusual
the most loving
Self

Collection of love thoughts and love dreams for sale
Auction opens today
The fastest one wins!

11,000 YEAR OLD WALL PAINTING FOUND

Have you heard?:

French archaeologists have discovered an 11,000-year-old wall painting underground in northern Syria. Rectangles dominate the ancient painting, which formed part of an adobe circular wall of a large house with a wooden roof.

"This site is one of several Neolithic villages in modern day Syria and southern Turkey. They seem to have communicated with each other and had peaceful exchanges," Coqueugniot said.

Mustafa Ali, a leading Syrian artist, said similar geometric design to that in the Djade al-Mughara painting found its way into art throughout the Levant and Persia, and can even be seen in carpets and kilims (rugs).

We have been creating art for at least 11,000 years and we still believe that our era is the 'special' one...

**when breathing disappears
and only sounds of Gods are heard
i'll give you my heart
completely**

EVERY CHILD COUNTS

My beloved Dun George
Moves swiftly through the crowds
With a smile of the enlightened few
and says - every singe child, but every single one - counts...

While we all struggle with our little unimportant Self-s
He runs mind-boggling number of projects

Thousands are fed and educated in his 160 homes
In Brazil, in Kenya and in Ethiopia

With sparkling eyes, he goes around saying:
-Nobody's child but everybody's children-
and taps my hand gently
bringing the air of inspiration and love

Thousands helped by this gentle-man...

Written in his diary while he was in Ethiopia:
*I met a sad young boy, next to a grave, and when I asked him who lays
there he answered: 'Baba a che nindo oko kacha': My father fell asleep
here, but he never woke up again!*

Learning the essence
of the 4th
Sacred Path
that is
shortest
driest &
the most dangerous one

SECRET

I am not quite sure but
there is a Word I am searching for today

a word of sorrow or a word of joy

a word of love or a word of hate

I know it is there - I saw its tale and horns and marrow

I hear it knocking - passing the sound

of Enlightenment? of Life? of Hope?

of Moksha - not Mukti!

of Nivana's glow?

of 1000s of Lung Ta flying in the air?

of mantras and yantras repeated for eons by many monks?

of the Divine Head and Her five nectars

of awakening of Sushumna Nadi

through Purification & Ecstasy

to Unity of Shiva and Shakti

with Cosmic Consciousness

IT IS IN YOU

It is the same drive
That gives both of us happiness
In this world of constant searches and nowhere to find drills
It is in progesterone, and testosterone
It is in your and mine brain
That are wired so differently &
Are in sync so beautifully
It is within the desert sand & stormy waters
It is in the depth of the blue
It is in the depth of you

It is in the depth of falling

And getting caught at the very last moment

FIRE DRAGON

I have seen the Ocean open
when you raised the stick

I have seen the Mountains move
when you looked up
& whispered - move

I have seen miracles
waiting to happen
hidden
in her contagious laughter
& I saw you lift her vale of secrets
to deliver
a thought
of deep blue waters
of silence that is only found
in the noises of nature
of shaking earth
that was touched
by the breath of
fire dragon
in love

SHAKTI DANCE

Universe was revolving in me
disguised as a thought foot-print
hiding a tide of God
borrowed from the sea
a question
Why?

Amidst the journey - Amin cracked the clouds
Amin - of Her Will

Stubbornness of Love rebelled
hold-on the Mighty-One
Hold-on!

Are we allowed just to taste it & not to live it?
Are we allowed just a glimpse of Her shadow?
Hold-on!

All the demons of life and
Thoughts - that we are buried under
Against Her supreme manifestation
Against Her Majesty awakened state
Against Her abode on Earth

What I dared I wished
What I wished I lived
Can I live It Again?

NOTRE DAME

A phantom serpent uncurls
at the bottom of my spine
to reveal
a perfection of **God's & Man's creation**
in the middle of Salsbourg Cathedral of Notre Dame

within a pure cup of **white Chinese tea**
that brews twice the drip of the sand dial on my table

within the hills of south German villages
and **meditation chair** that waits for me every morning
as though it was designed for me & my little visit

within the **eyes of an old lady** that starts chatting
as soon as she meets my eyes in the middle of the train

within hugs and kisses of mothers and children
connecting deeply with no words between them

a **perfection of God's & Man's creation**

HER MAJESTY WISDOM

Fate like a jackal feeds amongst
the tombs of past beliefs
digging deep into the wounds
of what you and me once called hope

I pondered sometime
at my first glimpse of the Temple
of human flash, of burning hearts
of confused whispers and determined sights

We all know the road - it is so clear
from the bottom of the spine
to our ancestor's accumulated wisdom
to love that has no lines, has no ends

We can take it in - I promise - try!
the magic and mystery hidden
within the walls of two that are many
scratch the surface, break into its core

What is our Goddess's name?
Where does the secret sleep?
Is it within the Stone?
Or Sun?
Or Sea?
With the minds of two, can we dream to comprehend
Her message of many?

TO A SPIRITUAL WARRIOR

God, Allah, Jahweh, Brahman, Tao **I am calling you**!!!

Unite with Emptiness
The One that already Is All

To True Nature   Ultimately Reality Essence of the Centre

Oooo, Infinite Empty Consciousness
Be my Mind   That always knew & always **Is**

END OF VIOLENCE

I believe, with all my being, that it is possible to end violence.

Completely.

Suffering can be healed.
It is our choice to have the violence, and
We can chose to live without it.

Completely.

One by one, our choices became our current reality.
With Intention and Conscious Choice
One by one, we create a new reality.

Reality without violence
Reality of New Earth
Of the Radiant Light of Cosmic Unconditional Love

Clouds
Spiritual cousins of
Elephants
Cross the plain gently
Leaving me in wonder about
Life and rain

LIFE PRAYER

May I be Eternal Consciousness
Aware and alert at every point

Of this cyclical existence

May I expand like a space
Absorbing the great elements

Earth & water & air into my being

May I always support

The **Life** and its manifestation

The **Growth** and its beauty

And the boundlessness of this creation

HIS CONSCIOUSNESS

To **Glorious Wisdom of Love**
To the **Profound Heart Sound**
To **Great Awareness** of the enlightened few
To **Limitless Space of Compassion**
To **Alertness of Bliss and Emptiness**

To Mind riding on the Wind of Light
To Amitaba and Amideva
To Milarepa and Baba Ji
To you my Father and Mather
Whose Merge brought me here
To experience
The Diamond Being
Within the Primeordial Consciousness
of One

BUDDHA MIND

It is so vast
    I can feel It
        Expanding
            Exploding
                Exploring
                Every call of my body

It is so vast
    I entered It
        And
            It left me
            Broken
            1,000,000s of pieces

It is so vast
    Without time
        Without space & essence
            It has never begun
            And will never end
            Like an Orgasm that lasts for-ever

∞ Like the Universe
In a grain of sand

Like Light Love   Movement   Silence
Within my DNA   In between two breaths

Like Death giving birth to Life

Like you and me in my dreams

ABYSS OF SHADOWS

My bird keeps flying directly towards my cat
she comes to me only when the cat is in my lap
she lands exactly where the cat sleeps
she exits her nest only when she hears the cat purring

Yesterday I saved her from the cat's jaws - will she learn?

or will she stay flying towards the deadly embrace
over-and-over-again
choosing a completely un-fair fight over her deepest fears

will she burn sacrificing her fragile body
within the same attraction
a butterfly suicidaly enters a flame

or will she learn to live
with her hypnotic fascination
in the same way
we - mortals - can learn to live
with our fascination
with light
keeping our journey
towards the death
long and intense
walking the edge
but not falling
into the abyss of its shadows

Now is Eternal
Born before its birth
Intelligence of equilibrium
We speed up Universal growth
Bringing Earth's future into the moment of Now

Seeking Direct, Clear Connection
to the very Source

SPOON OF HOPES

Silence gathered like clouds
around my arms, chest and throat
I picked it up with a spoon of hopes
that it will last for-ever

Spirits made to shine enter my mind
Leaving traces of our eternal dreams
Connect me to ME without ends

Instantly healed I chose my paths
With eyes closed and heart open
With no hesitation

I dreamt of a man
that was lost in his dream
not realising I was dreaming

Feelings café

Within the feelings café
we drunk a coffee of compassion
that brought us back
to our purpose
on this little blue planet

WALKING THE MILE

Walking the mile
I discovered
Ama's Temple in Macao
Lotus House in Malta
Himalaian Buddhist Monastery in Nepal
Hare Krishna Ashram in Belgrade
Ananda Marga's Jakriti in Singapore
Komaja's Heaven in Ibiza
Sivananda Yoga Centre in Madrid
House of God's Friends in New Zealand
Krishna's abode in India
Krishnamurti's Library in Cambridge
Gaia's abode in Findhorn

Treasuries of Wisdom
All over the world
hidden from the passers-by
available only to the few
who have eyes to see and
ears to hear
One Message
For All

I am Love that Knows
That there are no Lonely Pillars
As long as the Dome is within the Heart

FORCE OF LIFE

**Defining the intention
of our heart's desire
we discover
the Force of Life**

Lemon trees
and a cat stretching
under a bench
on a white step
at a street corner

Open with Touch of Consciousness

A world full of impressions
a world full of light
hidden within the hurry
of a non-believer

VISION OF A WISARD

How many of you wish to be Wizards when you grow old?

How many of you want to fly?

I wished to become a dragon – he said
And he looked at us with eyes filled with fire

The Wizard of Earth's Sea
Descended to tell us a secret of
ABRACADABRA
Get to know – he said - God's true name

The word will initiate Power
Gate keepers of Ancient Knowledge
Will open their doors
Mythological Archetypes will start their dance
Leading you to your tribal clout

Skeletons scattered over the burial grounds
Ancestors with their weapons and spears
Saints and Demons
Doctors and Gypsies
Healers and Witches
Will join you to celebrate

The Birth of Self
Power of Mind over Body
The Vision of the Dominion of Light

KUNDALINI DANCE

Dark and cold and wet were Her hands
I felt Her chilly breath inside my throat
Her claws deep inside trying to find traces of
Fear within me

I stayed still Accepting Opening Receiving

Within a moment She was inside
Two fingers below My belly button

In there She found no traces of shivers
no traces of resistance, no traces of weakness
just clear pure Passage-Way

Then She grew into Her most powerful Self
She stood undisturbed, unmoved, unchanged
Totally free and She screamed

AAAAAUUUUUUMMM

From the centre of the earth, Through the tunnels of the caves, To the
surface of the volcanoes
AAAAUUUUUUMMMM

To open: Mountain tops untouched by clouds and rain
Cherry fields in their full blossom

A dog running after a train filled with the excitement
A witch laughing at passers-by mirroring their paranoia
Death looking us in the eyes searching for the chosen Few Capable to
see the Key behind Her magic veil

@

**Living in the Rhythm of Now
gives us
An Abundance of Opportunities**

DIVINE INTENTION

**This is a spring of your desire
let Her come out into the Light
in Her best dress
of Divine Intention**

We do not source Power
We invite it in

I invite you - Power

Breaking spells that had their use

*Releasing Freedom,
Merging Left and Right
For the benefit of All*

A MESSAGE FROM A FRIEND

Please don't be sad.

Sorry if I am a pain. I can't help it as I was dropped on my head when I was a baby. Then I was abandoned in a dark forest by my wicked step mother and left to live with the wolves. Then I was turned into stone for a few years by an errant Medusa. Then I nearly got put in an oven by a wicked witch who fattened me up with sweetbreads. Then I got put in a dungeon with an iron mask for 25 years until my beard was as long as my arms.

But.. then I met you and became happy!

So if you are unhappy, then all these bad memories come back! So please S

A sigh of weeping willow

Landed onto my palm today
It got lost on its journey

From one dimension to the next
Searching for happiness

PLATO CAVE

In Plato's cave, prisoners are chained in a cave facing a wall, unable to turn their heads. Imagine, walking down a long dark cave that is turned into prison. And imagine at the end of it, you come across a wall in front of which on a stone bench sit people chained to each other and chained to the bench and they sit there living their lives day after day not being able to turn or move. Behind them burns a fire and puppeteers hold the puppets that cast shadows on the wall of the cave. The prisoners look at the shadows, observe their movements, believing that what they see is real. A shadow of a book is a book for them, a shadow of a chair is a chair for them and because that is the only reality that exists for them - they believe in it full-heartedly.

And after you have imagined all of this ask yourself: How much time in life I spend really feeling, seeing, hearing, tasting - really living, and how much do I spend observing the movements of the shadows on the wall in front of me?

How many hours of the day we spend passively chained to the chairs of our choosing and how many we spend running in the woods?

In AoL Mindfulness process we are connecting our individual stories with collective story bringing to our senses this model of collaboration in which we all have equal voice, even goals.

According to Greek creation myths Chaos (Greek: χάος, khaos) is the initial "gap" created by the original separation of heaven and earth. This disorder is beginning of creation, place to search for inspiration.

In modern world Chaos is a gap in creativity, disharmony between science and art, rational and irrational, the world of reason and the world of emotions, the gap we are trying to bridge, to unite by our organization.

Project Definition

Some 750 million adults – two thirds of them women – remained illiterate in 2016. Half of the global illiterate population lives in South Asia, and a quarter live in sub-Saharan Africa. Many developing countries still lack basic infrastructure and facilities to provide effective learning environments. Sub-Saharan Africa faces the biggest challenges: at the primary and lower secondary levels, less than half of schools have access to electricity, the Internet, computers and basic drinking water.

The growing breach between the rich and poor countries has not been met with the response of an equivalent flow of international solidarity. Global ecological and economic interdependence requires effective international cooperation for appropriate management. The inadequate cooperation of all countries is responsible for the continuing rivalries and inequities in the global economic and social system.

Using AoL European Mindfulness as a process, a philosophy and a methodological framework for the realization of collaborative and sustainable projects, we facilitate diversity, creativity and team-work around the Globe. The idea is to enlighten collective intelligence and unleash our creative genius working with many transformative projects and organisations across the world...

The series by Artof4Elements is inspired by Ancient Greek philosophers, symbolism and art, yin and yang, by mythology, alchemy, and within the parenting world by simplicity parenting, and alternative teaching educational models.

ABOUT THE AUTHOR Nataša Pantović

MSc (Master) Economics, Maltese Serbian Management Consultant, Adoptive Parent and Ancient Worlds' Consciousness Researcher.

Born in 1968, in Belgrade, Serbia, using stories of ancient Greek and Egyptian philosophers and ancient artists, after being Head of Business Development, Consultant and Trainer, for 20 years, of 4 largest consulting and IT companies in the UK, Holland, and Malta, Deloitte, KPMG, MEU - Government Consulting Agency, and Reeds Consulting, I inspire researchers to reach beyond their self-imposed boundaries.

Volunteering, I have organized 6 large Body, Mind and Spirit Festivals, I have provided panels for the International Vegetarian Festival, 10 days Conference about Neolithic Temples, and have represented Malta's IT outsourcing, all around the planet, including being on the Panel of Speakers within the Economist Mediterranean Business Summit in Marseille, France.

Published author since 1991, with a legal book on Co-operatives, I have helped build a school in a remote village of Ethiopia, and have since adopted two kids, as a single mum: check out our unusual story! In the last five years, with Artof4Elements, have published 2 historical fictions and 7 non-fiction books.
At the moment, I am fascinated by the research into Ancient Europe's Consciousness and Art. Applied Psychology and Philosophy of Languages, to deeper understand Intuitive Wisdom and Pure Ratio, through the Power of Mind.

www.ingramcontent.com/pod-product-compliance
Lightning Source LLC
Chambersburg PA
CBHW020116180626
46812CB00006B/2617